Valery stood by the doorway, blinking her eyes in the half-light, finding the thin, delicate figure standing in the center of the floor. The child's hair and alabaster skin seemed to glow.

"Tansy, please don't disappear like that again," Valery said.

"I didn't disappear. I came in here," Tansy replied. "Come in. Isn't it nice in here?"

Valery stepped inside and the pungent odor of wet, rotted wood and decaying leaves assailed her. She saw Tansy move lightly across the sagging floor, halting beside the huge water-wheel, then disappearing from sight around the other side. "Tansy, wait," Valery cried ... hurrying after the child.

Suddenly she felt the plank give under her foot, heard the sound of the splintering wood a split-second after and then she was falling, screaming out in terror ....

THE DARK MILL

CLAUDETTE NICOLE

CUTTING EDGE

ISBN-13: 978-1-957868-27-1

Published by
Cutting Edge Books
PO Box 8212
Calabasas, CA 91372
www.cuttingedgebooks.com

THE DARK MILL

CHAPTER ONE

Nobody had come.

It had been a month now, and no one had come, not even the child.

Except for the houseman, Labat—and just the thought of him sent a shudder through the girl's slender frame—she was still alone, alone with the cavernous old house in this strangely silent hollow of land. The afternoon had turned gray and wrapped itself in a chill wind again and the girl stood at the edge of the lake where the wind blew without ever rippling the water and the trees grew to the very edge of the shore. Her tall, willowy body an echo of the cattails that waved gracefully nearby, Valery Curtis scanned the stillness with her violet eyes, her hair jet black and shoulder length, blowing softly. She sank down on the grass, the edges of it stiff and unfriendly against her bare legs. The wind stabbed at her again. It was a strange place, this hollow of land, the girl thought once again. Beauty here was an ominous thing, at once frightening and compelling. At times she found herself one with the aloneness of it but today, in the grayness, she wished the others would come. There'd been no reason why they hadn't come, no word given why the child hadn't arrived weeks ago as was the arrangement, only the houseman's muttered assurance that "they will come."

A sudden movement interrupted her thoughts and she saw a giant diving beetle light on a fragment of floating water lily. The huge insect, glistening, wholly predatory, its powerful cutting jaws protruding from its broad head, sat unmoving and then Valery saw the tadpole wriggling its way along the shoreline. Almost a frog, with fully fleshed-out hind legs, the tadpole swam in small circles, moving nearer the beetle in slow unawareness. Valery looked away as the tadpole retreated, going off in the other direction. The giant beetle stayed unmoving, waiting, even as she sat and waited. Valery frowned; it hadn't been at all what she had expected, she reflected angrily, and she still saw the bitter, fearful faces of the townspeople when she'd arrived. None would take her to the hollow and she was despairing when Labat drove up in the vintage Ford. The townspeople's dark frowns had reminded her of her father's when she had told him of her plans, and, as Valery stared into the unruffled water, it became a mirror. She saw the tall, patrician figure of her father in it, standing in the living room of the handsomely furnished apartment; he was always contained, composed, even when he was hurt. She'd always thought him above being hurt until one day, with a secret delight, she'd found out differently.

The water moved to her left and she glanced up to see the tadpole had returned to playfully dive and surface in ever-widening circles. The huge, powerful beetle waited motionlessly. Her father was waiting, too, she knew, and in the water she saw him again, his aristocratic face unable to hide his hurt.

"It's no job for you," he had said. "You're only taking it because you know it will displease me."

"Nonsense," she had said coolly. "It's a chance to do something different and be paid for it and to get away."

She had met his stare, ashamed of how she enjoyed what she saw in his eyes.

"You won't give at all, will you?" he had said that evening. His eyes probed, and she reflected how vulnerable we are when we seek.

"I don't know what you mean. Let's not have a scene, Father," she had replied.

"The dinner was last night," he'd thrown back at her, more pain than reproach in his voice. "You could have come."

"I had a date. I told you that."

"A totally unimportant date. We both know that. This was the society's tribute to my work, a once-in-a-lifetime thing. You knew that, too."

Of course, she'd known that, the girl admitted. Robert Curtis had been one of the country's most respected architects for many years and his retirement had brought a small deluge of dinners and awards.

The water moved and Valery saw the tadpole come closer to the lily pad. The huge beetle remained absolutely motionless.

"You should have been there," her father had gone on. "It would have been proper, of course. But more important, it would have said something else. I looked for you, hoped to see you."

Valery had shrugged, ignored the pain in his eyes, and thought of all the times she had looked for him and hoped to see him, of uncounted disappointments that made all the best schools and all the right functions so empty and incomplete.

The water stirred again closer, and Valery saw the tadpole nearer to the lily pad. She caught the almost imperceptible movement of the beetle's deadly pincers. Letting the ominous tableau hang in the corner of her eye, she heard her father's voice again, and her classically beautiful face of perfect angles tightened in anger.

"I wonder if you'll ever understand," he had said. "When your mother was alive it was different. I left certain things for her to give. I had a career to build."

The defensive note in his voice was abrasive, angering. "Some things aren't to be delegated," she had snapped. "They die when you do."

"You learn that in time," her father had said. "You learn where you've been wrong. You learn and try to find a new way."

"Do you? Or do you just suddenly start needing?"

"Are you so preoccupied with paying back, Valery?" he had asked.

She had made an angry denial and, of course, she'd been doing exactly that, surprising herself at how much pleasure she derived from revenge. She was frightened by the depth and power of her feeling, and it was one of the reasons she welcomed getting away. She needed time and distance to put an end to something that was beginning to dominate her and that, for all the pleasure it gave her, made her uneasy with herself.

She saw the beetle suddenly raise its body, poise itself as a diver poises on a diving board. The tadpole was close to the lily pad now, still swimming in unconcerned circles.

"You'll be a glorified domestic," her father's voice came to her. He'd tried to hurt, but his attempts were born of needing and wanting and so they were weak.

"Good try," she had smiled thinly. "Thoroughly inaccurate but effective. But then you've always been more interested in effect than in anything else, haven't you?"

She had watched him struggle to make his pride mask the pain. Rejection brought rejection, she had reflected. An eye for an eye. Why was satisfaction so discomforting, she remembered wondering angrily. Why was victory so distasteful?

The tadpole had reached the lily pad, Valery saw, swimming lazily, idly. The beetle seemed lifeless, a shape on a leaf.

"I'm accepting the job," she had thrown out at her father, enjoying the defeat in his eyes.

The beetle dived, almost too fast to see, a flashing movement in the air and then cutting, killer pincers were slicing into the soft flesh of the tadpole. In split seconds death had ended life, pain had triumphed over pleasure, defeat over victory. The waters closed together and it was over.

Valery rose, her lips compressed into thinness and she looked up at the gray sky and listened to the silence. All of it for nothing? The question hung. Nobody had come yet. Perhaps nobody would. Perhaps there'd been a change in plans. There was mockery in the thought. Her father would have won after all and all the knife-edged words would have been better left unsaid. Perhaps that would have been better anyway. She stretched and shook her head trying to shake away the restlessness inside herself. She had tried to use the silence and the time to probe herself, to try to sift apart the emotions called love and cruelty, kindness and bitterness, and find out why they could so easily slip into each other. But it hadn't worked. The long month had given her only an increasing edginess. Only the Wheatens had helped; their cottage a discovery she'd made on one of her solitary walks beyond the confines of the hollow. Frances Wheaten was not much older than herself. Her husband, Fred, a quiet, friendly man, was a carpenter by trade. The cottage had been a help on the very lonely days, and the mile walk had been well worth it.

Valery started back up the gentle slope that led from the lake, leaving the silence of it behind. But then the lake was hardly more silent than the rest of the hollow. In the month she'd been there she hadn't heard a bird sing. None of the small woodland creatures scurried about, not a chipmunk or a hedgehog, not even a squirrel. Yet the grass was thick, the foliage lush. But only insects moved in the hollow. As she reached the top of the incline, she turned onto the road and started back toward the house. The land rose softly to the right, fringed with trees and bordered with gentians. Beyond them, dropping quickly, lay the swamp, always mist-shrouded, no matter what time of the day she had paused at its edge. Lifeless, twisted trees rose from the mists and pitcher plants thrust upward, flesh-eaters of deadly deception. It had a compelling voraciousness to it, the misted bogs and silent trees almost inviting in a macabre way. On the left, the grass grew in broad sweeps dotted with orange milkweed. As the road neared the house, the wild tansy grew in profusion on both sides: it was easy to see why the child had been named for this plant.

The road dipped, then rose and the house came into view, the exterior of it a hideous mélange of Jacobean and French Renaissance, of deeply recessed doorways and projecting bays, of dark wood piled atop dark wood, of gabled roofs burdened with ornamented woodwork. The interior was still worse, so overcarved, so overfurnished and heavy with baroque trappings as to be almost obscene. It sat in the center of the hollow like a giant squash grown overripe and turning with decay. As she neared the heavy-sided monstrosity of a house, Valery thought of Carlotta Van Dyne. The old dowager was the reason she was here at this place of strange silences.

Valery's hospital work had been voluntary, in between jobs, and Carlotta Van Dyne's room had been one she passed scores of times each day on her rounds with the book and magazine cart. The old woman had been easy to talk to, an old dowager of commanding presence even in hospital robes, eyes snappingly bright in a face that was saved from being crone-like by a touch of imperiousness. The woman had been there for over a month, hospitalized by a heart condition. Daily stops with the cart in her room turned into after-work visits as Carlotta Van Dyne turned out to be a persuasive, arresting person. She could fascinate by the accuracy of her probes, Valery learned, and she had an uncanny ability to touch on the troubled places of the inner heart. Valery found herself telling Carlotta Van Dyne things she had held close to herself, of secret resentments and unhappinesses, of disillusions with a very practical world that the finest of schools had done little to prepare her for.

During one such long visit Carlotta Van Dyne had made the offer. "You need something to help you find yourself, a challenge, and you need to get away by yourself," the old dowager had said. "I've just the thing for you, managing my granddaughter for two months."

Valery had frowned. *"Managing* your granddaughter?"

"Yes, she's a most independent child and in need of management," the old woman had answered. "Oh, you'd be well paid. Three thousand dollars for a two-month period and all your living expenses."

"You take my breath away," Valery recalled saying.

"I think you have what the child needs," the woman had mused. "Youth, energy, education, imagination. And I think you could cope with the others."

"The others?"

"Yes, my sons and whatever guests they may bring with them at the same time my granddaughter is delivered from the summer school she attends. You'd go to our family home, *Verdelet*. It's at the very tip of Maine, right on the borderline where New Brunswick and the end of the Gaspé and Maine meet in a triangle. We've a houseman, Labat, who will do all the domestic work. Your concern would be the child's welfare and standing in for me as hostess. I never know who may come along at this time and I'm just not physically up to the task. My doctor insists I take a long, quiet rest."

"Why not just tell everyone that?"

"And have them not come? Oh, no, my dear, that would never do. It's a family tradition to get together once a year at this time. The child's birthday is celebrated, too. Her parents were killed when she was four, a family tragedy. So everyone looks forward to these reunions. No, it would never do to call it off. But this year they'll do without me, if you'll accept, of course."

Carlotta Van Dyne had gone on to tell her more about the job and the essential simplicity of it. She'd even warned of the unfriendliness of the people of the *Lac Long* region, but Valery had not expected quite the coldness of the greeting she had gotten in town. Mostly, though, it sounded like a wonderful, paid vacation and she had virtually agreed before mentioning it to her father. She'd known what his reaction would be, of course, and known it would make her decision that much more final.

The road brought her abreast of the house, and she strode on more quickly, angrily. It hadn't turned out at all as she expected, certainly not yet. Despite the fact that the money had been deposited in her account in advance, she had decided now to leave if there was no word by the end of the week. She'd return the money to Carlotta Van Dyne when she got home. The chill wind whipped her hair and she fought off a shiver as she strode past the heavy, overhanging entranceway that threw a shadow in front of it. She glimpsed the houseman, Labat, standing in the doorway, his cadaverous face unsmiling as always, his apelike arms hanging from the sleeveless jacket he wore. She felt his eyes on her as she strode past the house. She walked on, over the small rise and then the larger one that marked the end of the hollow. The road wound ahead of her and she walked on until, beside an arched trio of silver birches she turned and went into the woods, emerging into a small glen hidden from the road. She saw Fred Wheaten's pleasant face look up to greet her.

"God, it's good to see you today," Valery breathed, letting out an irritated sigh.

"One of the edgy days, was it?" he said, and Valery sank down on a length of log. She saw Fred's toolbox nearby, the long saws sticking from one end of it, as if proclaiming his work as a carpenter. Every afternoon for the past two weeks they had met like this, in the glen, as though they were lovers.

"Do you think anyone would believe I've been giving you French lessons?" she had quipped one afternoon and seen Fred Wheaten redden at once.

"As soon as I'm ready to surprise Fran we'll meet at the house," he had said quickly, and she had laughed at his obvious embarrassment. It had all started when he'd learned that she had majored in French and, excited at once, he'd taken her aside during one of her visits to the cottage.

"Fran can speak French," he had said proudly. "Real good, too, I've been told. She's had a lot more education than me but then that's easy enough to see, isn't it? But I'd like to surprise her. If you could teach me enough to really surprise her, I'd keep it up. Fran'd help me."

He had had the simple eagerness of the honest, humbly unashamed, and she'd agreed at once and the secret meeting place had been decided upon. As the weeks went by and the child still didn't come, she had grown more and more grateful for the daily lessons in the little glen. They helped her to live with the mounting uneasiness and tension that settled on her. And in the little glen an oriole or a thrush was certain to sing. Only a quarter-mile from the hollow, it seemed a different world.

"Every afternoon it gets chillier," Valery commented, shivering. "Let's get started. I don't know how many more lessons there'll be."

"You going to leave, Valery?" Fred asked, his wide, affable face looking as concerned as it could look. She smiled grimly.

"If no one arrives by the weekend," she said. "I've just had it, I'm afraid, a case of too much solitude. Or maybe it's just that damned hollow where nothing ever moves or sings except insects. Or maybe it's Labat. The eeriness of the man could unnerve a stone statue. Or maybe it's just that suffocating house."

Or maybe a lot of things, she added silently, like having too many private wells of loneliness to cope with the force of this outside isolation. Shaking off the thoughts, she plunged into the day's lesson with a determined kind of relief. It was almost dark when they'd finished and Fred was pleased with his progress.

"Ready to surprise Fran?" Valery asked.

"A few days more," he said. "I want to be sure."

"A few days more," Valery laughed as they left the glen to push through the birches and onto the road.

"Come to dinner," Fred Wheaten said. "I think you could use the company. I'll tell Fran we met on the road and I invited you."

"Thanks, Fred, but I'll stick it out another night," Valery answered. The man shrugged and turned down the road. Valery watched him go, a guileless man without complexities. She shook off the chill and started back toward the hollow, hurrying in the last moments of day and wondering why she had refused the invitation. Another night in the tomblike silence of the house repelled her and yet she was drawn to the prospect as though an inner force demanded it of her. The challenge of it, she asked herself. Stubbornness? Or self-punishment? We are like single-celled creatures, she reflected, reacting to stimuli we do not consciously recognize, aware only of their existence, our psyches taking corrective action when touched. Quickly, angrily, she shut off her thoughts, unwilling to follow where they would surely lead her. The big house loomed ahead now, a black bulk with pinpoints of light from the foyer windows and the latticed panes of the dining room. As she passed the stables a few yards from the house she peered into the open doorway, barely able to make out the outlines of the four stalls. She heard the sound of the big, wild-eyed chestnut in the first stall. He had a distinctive habit of pounding his hooves on the floor, almost a drumbeat sound. She'd gone in to look at the place one afternoon and felt an intruder, the horses suddenly restless, disturbed by her presence. Usually she was good with horses and a fairly competent rider. Yet these steeds, especially the big chestnut, held a wildness that frightened, and she had left quickly. Labat kept them conditioned and groomed, and when she had asked him who rode them he had said only that they belonged to "M'sieu Bob." Now, with another quick glance, she hurried past the stables and into the house, straining to push open the thick, tall front door.

Verdelet had electricity through every room and there was a telephone in the study on the first floor. Yet hurricane lamps were everywhere and Labat seemed to prefer the kerosene lamps for he lit them every night. Passing the wavering light of a hall lamp, she mounted the wide, carpeted stairway to the second floor and her room, flicking on the light switch as she entered. It was a comfortable room, less overstuffed than the others. A large, canopied bed filled most of it and she had her own bath. She washed and went down to dinner without changing. As he had done every night since her arrival, Labat had a place set for her at one end of the long dining room and candles on the table. It was, as always, served on fine Wedgewood china of midnight blue with a white center and with a good, and correct, wine in a silver bucket. The big, gaunt-faced man moved in and out of the room on silent feet, almost magically appearing and disappearing into the far reaches of the huge room.

As she ate, grateful for the noises of the tinkle of silverware, the sound of the wine being poured, anything that helped to cut the silence, she wondered if this was how Carlotta Van Dyne ate every meal. The big room, paneled in dark wood, was hung with heavy-framed pictures, mostly muddy, chromatic landscapes and it seemed to close in on her as she hurried to finish the meal. She drained the wine as she had taken to doing every night. It helped make her comfortably drowsy and almost unmindful of the silence that could seep into the bone. Finished, Valery rose and went into the hallway, pausing in the uncertain light of the kerosene lamp on the wall mounting. She gazed down the long corridor at the protruding, wooden frames around each of the doors to the main rooms on the ground floor. Each entranceway was carved, curlicued, and ornamented, everything carried to excess, everything with one carving too many, one embellishment too much. It gave the house a feeling of silent turbulence, a place where all the hidden excesses of the soul could find expression. Certainly simplicity, purity, even laughter, seemed out of place here at *Verdelet*. She thought about the name as she mounted the stairs, noting again the elaborate *V* carved into the heavy cornerpost of the banister. It had a faintly French ring to it and yet the only word like it in French was a term for a wine that had not matured and was still heavy with acidity. Probably it was an ancestral name she had decided. Reaching her room, she slipped the latch on, noting again how ridiculously frail it was for so heavy a door. Yet she latched it at once.

One comfort the house boasted was good hot water and she filled the big, old-fashioned tub with it as she undressed. From her second-story window she could look over the crest of the rise, and though now it was dark, she could discern the blacker outline of the Notre Dame Mountains in the north. That would be the long finger of land that became the Gaspé to the northeast. Directly to the east were the gentler hills of New Brunswick. A book in the library had filled her in on the settlers of this triangle of land, this juncture of three provinces. On the border of the Gaspé, really Quebec Province, it had been mostly French peasant stock, close-mouthed, humorless people and in New Brunswick there had been both Scottish and French, the dourness of the Scots still part of the people. Maine itself had been settled here by those hardier, more iconoclastic members of the Puritans who brought their own unyielding ways with them, so *Verdelet* straddled what seemed to be a confluence of austerity. Perhaps it was only fitting that nothing warm sang or moved in the long hollow that was part of the land.

The bath, nearly ready, demanded her attention and she undressed quickly, her tall, lithe body briefly reflected in the long bathroom mirror as she stepped into the tub. She saw upturned breasts, firmly rounded, a small waist and long, slender legs, a body that was touched by the delicacy of a Degas. She sank into the bath, the water against her body sensuous, caressing, and she half smiled as her skin reacted to the heat and softness of the water. Maybe that was adding to her edginess. She was always a bit more on edge when she ended a relationship and that's what she had done with Ben Wright just before coming here. She always felt a little guilty, a little cruel, especially when she'd taken the initiative in ending it. She hated cruelty, abhorred being callous and yet she could be both. Her father had come to learn that, she knew, and so had Ben and others before him. Yet she couldn't be cruel, not really, she told herself. She'd only done what had to be done, said what had to be said. Truth, not cruelty. She clutched the thought to her with the haste of the uncertain.

Stepping from the tub, she dried herself, rubbing her skin pink, slipping on a terry cloth robe to pause at the window. Her eye caught the movement outside, and she discerned Labat's gaunt, angular figure crossing to the stables, long arms swinging loosely. She watched the houseman until he disappeared from sight and then she went to bed, letting her bare skin rub against the smoothness of the sheets. She lay there, listening to the silence, her thoughts turning in on herself. The month had been a waste. She'd wanted the catharsis of new work, of learning through doing, of stepping back from herself, even of contemplation. But there'd been none of that here, not in this overwrought, decadent mansion where not even the silence was peaceful. Sleep was a haven, a refuge from thinking, from feeling, from oneself, from waste. She let the unexplored images drift away in her mind and closed her eyes. They would be there, waiting for another time.

Valery slept soundly despite the number of times she turned and tossed, moonlight bathing her shoulders and breasts in silver. It was deep into the night, in the hushed hours, when she woke, rising on one elbow, frowning, listening. Something had wakened her. She listened and heard nothing. Straining her ears, she held her breath and listened again. There was nothing. No, Valery grimaced angrily, *not* nothing. There was *something*, unheard, not made of sound or sight, a presence, a feeling of something different in the house. Was she just imagining? She let herself sink down onto the bed, her lips drawn tight. Had she heard sounds, voices, or had she so wanted to that she'd dreamed them? It was all too possible, she knew, and she lay still, waiting, hoping for some small sound that would prove her right. But there was none. Dammit, she muttered silently. She hadn't wakened for no reason at all. There *had* been *something*. Unless, and she turned angrily in bed, it had been only her nerves after all, playing grim tricks on her. She buried her face in the pillow until sleep stole away her anger.

It wasn't till morning that she woke again, this time to the soundless warmth of the sun caressing her face. She sat up at once, and once again there was no sound, but she felt the same thing as she had during the night, the sense of something different in the house. Dressing quickly, she put on her gray skirt and deep red sweater, liking the way it clung to her. She unlatched the door as she gave her hair a last few strokes with the brush and then she was in the hall, starting down the wide stairway. She was halfway down when the figure moved into view, standing at the foot of the steps, looking up, unsmiling. Valery drew her breath in sharply.

"Tansy!" she exclaimed and practically flew down the remaining steps as the child, unmoving, watched her. Carlotta Van Dyne's description of the child had been wholly inadequate. Tansy, wearing a simple black dress with a white band at the collar, was a piece of Dresden china, a figurine of exquisite beauty, delicate, fragile. Hair of spun gold framed a face of perfect features and alabaster skin, her nose straight, thin, her lips soft-lined. But it was the child's eyes that held Valery at once, completely round, a pale, translucent, luminous blue, the eyes of a Siamese cat. In a shaft of sunlight from the hall window, the child shimmered with an evanescent beauty.

"You're Valery," the child said as the girl reached the bottom step, managing, somehow, to make the words sound slightly disdainful.

Valery smiled. "I'm no surprise to you, then." The luminous orbs were direct, unwavering, unblinking.

"Carlotta wrote me," the child said.

"I see," Valery said, her smile genuine, welcoming. "Do you always call your Grandmother Carlotta?"

"Everybody does," Tansy said.

"Well, now, when did you get here?" Valery asked.

"Last night. Late," Tansy said, and Valery felt the instant thought leap in her mind. Was that when she'd woken? Was that when she'd felt the strange presence in the house?

"I'm certainly glad you're here at last," Valery said, shunting aside the inner questions. "I was beginning to think you weren't coming at all."

"There was a delay," Tansy said, dismissing the remark, the disdain in her voice again. Valery told herself the irritation she felt was amusement.

"Then I take it you're all settled in your room," Valery said. "Labat told me it was the same room as mine, except in the east wing."

"That's right," Tansy said. The round, pale-blue eyes had still not blinked, Valery noted. There could be something disconcerting about their directness, she decided, and she turned away briefly.

"We've got to get acquainted, Tansy," she said. "Is there anything special you'd like to do today?"

"Go out walking. I know a lot of special places here in the hollow."

"All right. I've done quite a bit of walking about myself during the past month," Valery replied.

"Have you?"

The question was touched with faint amusement, and Valery looked down at the child. The luminous, round eyes were expressionless, returning her glance with unfathomable blandness. Tansy turned and headed for the door as Valery followed quickly. They were half-way out when the houseman appeared, his deep-socketed eyes on the child.

"We're going for a walk, Labat," Tansy said to the man. "I'll be back later."

"Yes, Miss Tansy," Labat said. There was a deference in his manner Valery hadn't seen before. "The others will be coming," Labat added. "They'll want to see you."

It was more than a statement of fact, more than a reminder. It held the faintest hint of reproof in it and the child paused to smile back at Labat. It was a smile that, somehow, didn't at all disturb the mask like calm of her face and that disappeared so quickly it almost might never have been.

"Then they should have been here," Tansy said to Labat, turning abruptly to go out the door. Valery followed, keeping the frown from her face with some effort. It had been a strange exchange with much left unsaid. Tansy's spun-gold hair was already bobbing along a good distance ahead and Valery hurried to catch up. As she did, Tansy's round, pale-blue eyes turned on her, and she thought she saw amusement with the touch of disdain in them. Certainly there was a cool aloofness in them, so she tried a smile. It got no reply and she fell in step with the child. Perhaps the child was masking a shyness, an uncertainty, with her coolness. It was not uncommon in children who were basically shy, who needed to be drawn out, she knew.

"Do you have many friends here, in the village, I mean, Tansy?" Valery tried.

"No," Tansy said softly. "Not anymore."

"Why not anymore? What happened?"

"I got tired of them."

Valery glanced at the child but the features remained perfectly calm. As they crested a small rise, Valery saw the bogs directly ahead of them, the mist shrouding them as always. They had come a way she had never used, approaching the swamp from another side. A cluster of tall, lifeless trees rose up together to fan out like a naked umbrella with only the ribs left.

"Where are we going, Tansy?" she asked.

The child's voice was soft, sing-song, almost as though she were speaking to herself. "Did you ever see a broken mill, an old dead fly on a water-wheel? Did you ever see the way things cling to what they used to be?"

Valery didn't try to hide her frown this time as she looked at the fragile beauty of the child. The translucent Siamese cat's eyes turned on her briefly and then looked away. She was a most unusual child, Valery concluded.

"We'll go through the bogs," Tansy said, nodding to the swamp only a few yards ahead now.

"Through the swamp?" Valery echoed.

"There's a way. I know it."

"Oh, no, Tansy, not in that mist," Valery said quickly. "Why, one wrong step might be fatal."

"I said I know a way," the child replied. Valery smiled again but it took more effort, and she wondered if Tansy was probing, testing, as children often do.

"No bogs," Valery answered flatly. "You must remember, Tansy, that I've been hired to look after you. I'm afraid we'll have to do things my way. I'm really quite easy to get along with and we'll have lots of fun but now that you're here you are my responsibility. Do I make myself clear?"

Tansy held her gaze for a moment, the blue eyes unfathomable, and then she shrugged.

"There's another path, a little longer," Tansy said flatly, starting off. The answer was neither an acceptance nor a challenge, not concession and not refusal, but Valery decided not to press further. The child was already halfway up a rise leading away from the bog and Valery hurried after her, finding herself on a pathway of shoulder-high reeds. She just managed to keep the spun-gold hair in sight as it bobbed along ahead of her. They were going deeper into the hollow, in a direction she'd never gone on her own and now the child's head disappeared from sight altogether for long moments.

"Tansy, wait," she called out, half-running through the tall reeds and thick grass. She felt the tension gathering inside herself. She was too wound up, too on edge, she reminded herself. The long month of wondering and waiting had done it, of course, and the child's sudden appearance was unnerving. Damn, she couldn't see the child at all now and she called out again. The child was eager or headstrong, or maybe a little of both. She pressed forward, running now, and then suddenly the tall reeds came to an end and before her stood an abandoned mill, a huge waterwheel taking up one end of it. The roof sagged and the walls leaned, but the waterwheel was intact. The child was nowhere to be seen, and she rushed forward, fearful and angry at the same time, forcing herself to slow down. Frightened anger was no answer. The child obviously knew her way around in the hollow, knew she could elicit a reaction of fear. Calm firmness was in order, Valery murmured silently. The old dowager had said the child was independent. The sagging old mill and the huge water-wheel were directly in front of her, the bottom quarter of the wheel hidden from sight as it dipped down into what once had obviously been a small stream running beneath the mill. One nail on one hinge held a side door hanging open and Valery stepped into the doorway, blinking her eyes in the half-light, finding the thin, delicate figure standing in the center of the floor. Even here, the child's hair and alabaster skin seemed to glow.

"Tansy, please don't disappear like that again," Valery said.

"I didn't disappear. I came in here," Tansy replied. "Come in. Isn't it nice in here?"

Valery stepped into the mill and the pungent odor assailed her at once. It was made up of wet, rotted wood and decaying leaves, moss and dank, sunless dampness. She saw Tansy move lightly across the sagging floor, halting beside the huge waterwheel.

"Look here, he's still there, the old dead fly," the child called and Valery felt her lips tighten as she moved forward. Tansy pointed to the side of one of the thick paddles where the huge horsefly lay, partly cemented to the wood by a white encrustation of fungi, grisly, repellent. Tansy, Valery noticed, looked at it almost lovingly.

"The stream still runs under the mill, mostly mud-water now," the child said, wheeling around in a circle. She disappeared from sight around the other side of the huge waterwheel and Valery called to her. "Tansy, wait," she cried, hurrying after the girl, but the child had vanished.

She saw the long, narrow walkway bordering the waterwheel on the other side, uneven wood planking that led to a thin, spiral stairway at the far end of it, hardly visible in the dimness. It obviously led up to another landing, and Tansy had apparently scurried up it. Dammit, Valery muttered silently. She'd have to put an end to this business of disregarding her. She hurried forward along the narrow walkway beside the giant, wooden wheel, stepping down hard in her haste, calling the child at the same time. She felt the plank give under her foot first, the sound of the splintering wood a split-second after and then she was falling, being pitched forward, screaming out in terror. It seemed agonizingly slow when it was all a matter of seconds as she felt her hand grasp onto the giant wheel, close around one of the inclined paddles at the top edge of it as she fell hard against it. Before she could regain her balance the wheel turned, the heavy paddle moving away under her grasp, and she felt herself falling, first against the paddle and then, as it turned under her weight, through the wide aperture between the paddles. She heard herself scream again as, clutching out, her arms flailing against the wood, she was thrown forward and through the paddles. Her hand caught at a thick edge only to slip off and she twisted her body sideways, striking her shoulder against the edge of the waterwheel as it slowly turned and then she was falling sideways, banging once more against the turning wheel as she hit bottom, the fall somewhat cushioned by the dark stream of shallow water and the soft mud bottom under it.

Reacting instinctively, she rolled sideways against the stone side of the mill as the paddles of the waterwheel came down. She felt heavy, wood paddles brush against her back as she pressed herself against the stone, letting the first one pass, then half-turning to look up behind her. The wheel was turning, slowly, thank God, yet slowly was all too fast as the next paddle loomed above her. As it came down, she flung herself against the wall again to let it brush by her. Despite its slowness, turning more on its own momentum than by the power of the sluggish few inches of water in which she lay, she knew the weight of the huge paddles could crush her skull in like an eggshell. Another came down to brush past her, this one a hair's breadth wider, scraping along her back. When it passed she half-turned again and glanced down the narrow bed of the stream where the mill had been built over it to house the bottom part of the wheel. If the wheel could be halted she could crawl out from her corner beneath it to emerge at the end of the short housing. Another paddle came down and she barely managed to turn back against the stones in time.

"Tansy!" she screamed. "Tansy! Down here, beneath the waterwheel."

She knew her body hurt and she tasted blood on her lips but desperation pushed all else but survival aside. She couldn't keep avoiding the heavy paddles. Sooner or later she'd slow down and be struck the crushing blow.

"Tansy!" she screamed again as a paddle brushed past her. Turning as it went by, feeling the pain of her shoulders, she heard the sound of movement above her and through the spaces between the paddles she glimpsed the spun-gold hair and the fine-featured head peering down from the walkway.

"Stop the wheel, Tansy," Valery said, her phrases bursting out in a race against the next descending paddle. "Push a board into it. Stop it from turning."

She'd no time for more instructions as the paddle came down on her and she flung herself against the stones once again, feeling the heavy wood brush her hair this time.

"There's nothing long enough up here," she heard the child say, her voice sounding terribly distant. "It'll have to stop by itself. It always does in time."

In time, Valery echoed silently. Her body was quivering now, her muscles hardly responding. In time would be too late. Her only chance was to get out from where she was trapped beneath the turning wheel and reach the end of the housing. Silently, she counted as one of the heavy paddles brushed by her, one, two, three, four, five, six, seven, eight, nine ... nine seconds before the next paddle brushed against her. She had nine seconds to crawl from her position and be far enough along the stream bed to avoid being crushed by the next paddle. Nine seconds to turn from the stone wall, turn onto her stomach and crawl. It wasn't enough, not on hard ground and certainly not in this soft mud that would cling to her. Nine seconds. Not enough and yet it had to be enough. She felt her body quivering as her muscles began to give out in the cramped, twisted position against the stones of the wall. Another paddle brushed by, and she gathered herself, feeling her body shake from the cold, slime-covered wetness of her clothes. The next paddle was passing, brushing her with its leading edge and then, as it started on its upward turn, she flung herself from the wall, twisting her body as she did so. She landed face down, her feet churning, digging into the muddy water, pushing herself forward. Her knees sank into the soft bottom of the stream bed and, clawing with her hands, she pulled herself onward. Then she felt the sweep of air behind her as the next paddle descended. With a last, desperate thrust, crying out as she did so, she threw herself forward in the muddy streamlet as the paddle brushed across her legs, nudging her rear, and went on. Sobbing, she lifted her head and crawled forward to the end of the housing, pulling herself up onto the grass that sloped down to the sluggish water where the stones ended.

She lay there, her breath coming in great gasps, her body aching in pain and shaking. The grass against her face felt good, dry and comforting, and she was alive, she repeated to herself, alive. Her gasping breaths finally stopped and her shaking body halted itself and she lay quietly, suddenly aware that she was not alone. Turning her head, gasping with the pain of pulled muscles, she saw the child standing there, looking down at her, contained, immaculate, infuriatingly calm.

"What happened?" she heard Tansy's voice asking.

"A board gave way," Valery gasped, spitting out mud and slime. "On that catwalk. I fell into the wheel and it pitched me down under it."

The effort to explain was exhausting and she fell silent, struggling for breath. She heard the child's words almost unbelievingly.

"You'll have to be more careful, won't you?" she heard Tansy say sweetly and she looked up at the child, her own eyes narrowing. The Dresden china figurine was made of cold steel inside. That, or there were psychic blocks which prevented the normal, emotional reactions.

"Yes," Valery said slowly. "I'll have to be more careful."

"Shall I get Labat?" the child asked, the disdain in her voice again. Valery felt her lips tighten in anger and she started to pull herself to her feet, ignoring the sharp pains that shot through her back and shoulders.

"No, I'll make it back," she said. "We'll have to go slowly, that's all."

She looked up from one knee, saw Tansy shrug and watch her. She rose to her feet, swayed in dizziness for a moment and then, as her head cleared, she saw the half-dried streaks of blood on her arms from assorted cuts and scrapes. Glancing down, she saw she was caked with mud and she felt the thick dirt on her face. Every muscle crying out in protest, she started to follow the child back, wincing with each step. Tansy walked on ahead, not even glancing back at her, skipping, picking small yellow flowers, carefree, humming to herself, seemingly untouched by anything that had happened. Valery hobbled along after her, a grim anger keeping her moving forward, stumbling, crying out in pain, gritting her teeth and going on again. When the heavy, brooding face of the house came into view she was fighting off nausea as the pain now stabbed at her without halt. Tansy, nearing the house, ran ahead and Valery had no strength left to call out. She saw figures in front of the house. Or were they just imagined? The waves of nausea were making her dizzy. Tansy disappeared. The figures seemed to melt away, return to sight, run toward her. She swayed and the scene swam away as, with a last moment of consciousness, she felt herself collapsing, sinking to the ground.

CHAPTER TWO

S he woke in stages, conscious first of being less slime-covered, less caked with mud and then aware of hands on her, rubbing her back, hurting and helping at the same time. Her eyes opened and she saw the whiteness of a pillow in front of her. Lifting her head she started to turn, feeling the pain of the effort and the hands on her back draw away. A face materialized in front of her as she turned, like a picture on a screen being brought slowly into focus. She began to see black-brown eyes, dark, unruly hair, a straight nose and high cheekbones. It was a handsome face, intense, vibrant, electric.

"Hello, Valery," the face said and as she tried to sit up the hands were on her shoulders, gently but firmly pushing her back and now she realized that under the thin sheet that lay across her she was naked. Instinctively her hand clutched at the top of the sheet to draw it up as she rested on one elbow. The handsome, vibrant face broke into a quick smile that was instantly enveloping and she heard the low chuckle.

"Easy does it," the man said. "I'm Bob Van Dyne. I'm afraid you've had a rough one."

Valery managed a nod as she swallowed, her throat dry. The smile came again, lasting longer this time.

"After we carried you up here I took the liberty of cleaning you up a bit with a warm towel," Bob Van Dyne said and his eyes held a note of laughter combined with pleasure as his glance flicked down at the sheet that covered her.

"Thank you," she said. "My apologies. This is hardly the way to greet someone, is it?"

"I rather liked it," he grinned and his eyes moved down to where her breasts rose up from the edge of the sheet. She was surprised at the knot of malicious pleasure that stirred inside her. Beauty was its own weapon.

"You're a very beautiful girl," Bob Van Dyne said. "But I'm sure you've heard that before."

"One never tires of hearing that," Valery smiled, sinking down onto the bed. "I think I'm a very lucky girl, too," she added soberly. "I came awfully close to being killed this morning."

"Yes, from what I heard," Bob said and she saw his face stiffen. "A terrible experience." Then, his eyes brightening, he smiled and pressed his hand on her arm. "But you weren't killed and that's all that counts. Accidents will happen. This one turned out all right."

Valery studied the handsome man before her, his intense face reflecting an inner turbulence and she decided that he was exciting in a way different from any man she'd ever met. Even in repose, his eyes, his face, reflected a driving restlessness.

"I think that death never comes until one's time is up," he said. "It's as simple as that. No matter how we tempt it, it never happens till the time it's supposed to."

"A touch fatalistic, that," Valery answered.

"Perhaps." He shrugged.

The knock on the door intruded and Valery turned to watch the door open and another man enter as Bob called to him. "Glen, come on in," he said. "Our damsel in distress is feeling a little better."

The man came toward the bed, tall, dressed in a gray jacket and a turtleneck sweater. He was even-featured, attractive, with hazel eyes that were gentle. There was none of Bob Van Dyne's vital turbulence about him and he seemed colorless in contrast.

"This is Glen Perry," Bob introduced. "I brought him along with me as my guest. We work together and he's heard me mention *Verdelet* so often I decided he ought to spend some time here himself."

"Welcome," Valery said. "I'm certainly not being much of a hostess, am I?"

Glen Perry's smile was as gentle as his eyes and there was warmth and sincerity in his voice. He was instantly likable, Valery decided.

"I'm sure we can manage," he said. "You take things slow."

Valery shook her jet-black hair. "No, I'm really all right," she said. "A hot bath will make me feel a lot better. If you'll excuse me I'll get to that and be down to join you."

"Only if you promise to soak for at least an hour and then rest some more," Bob Van Dyne said. "Brother Martin hasn't arrived yet so there's only Glen and myself and Tansy. We'll see to her till you get down. Glen won't mind."

"No, not at all," Glen Perry echoed.

"All right," Valery said. "I'll be down later then."

"Good enough," Bob finished, getting to his feet. He was no taller than Glen Perry, she saw, but broader, slightly heavier. "You can play some lawn tennis with Tansy while I unpack," he said to Glen as they started for the door.

"Sure thing, whatever you say, Bob," Valery heard Glen answer, and then the door closed after them. One a vibrant, dominant personality, the other quiet, pliable, she mused. They complemented each other. She lay quietly for a few minutes, gathering herself, and then she got out of bed, every muscle of her body protesting. Her clothes were in a heap beside the bed, she saw, and she found herself wondering how long he'd let his eyes linger on her. Long enough, she decided, thinking of the rakish intensity of the man. Walking gingerly, aching with each step, she went into the bathroom and let the water into the tub as hot as she could stand it. Soaking in the heat, she let it seep into her until some of the throbbing was gone from her back and shoulders. Finally she stepped from the tub, wrapped in a towel, and lay down under the bed covers, half-sleeping, half-thinking, until she saw the shadows deepening in the room. She got up and dressed, feeling better. Passing the window, she looked outside in the half-light of dusk and saw Glen Perry's figure stroll around the corner of the stables.

The hall just outside her room was almost dark and she saw that Labat hadn't put on his kerosene lamps yet. But as she started down the steps, she saw the strong beam of electric light thrusting out from the library and she heard the voices, Labat's first.

"It was not my place to stop her," she heard him say in his deep growl.

"No, of course not, Labat, but Tansy knew better." It was Bob Van Dyne's voice, controlled anger in it. "Tansy knows very well what she's to do and not to do," he went on.

"You weren't here. I decided to go on my own." It was Tansy's voice and she heard the off-hand shrug in it.

"And do things your way before any of us got here," Bob's voice answered. "Well, there'll be no more of it, do you understand?"

The child was obviously being taken to task for what had happened at the old mill. A reprimand might well be in order, she reflected, but was it the best way to approach the child? She made a mental note to discuss Tansy with Bob and then she heard the front door open as Glen Perry entered the house. The conversation from the library halted abruptly and Valery went down the rest of the steps, reaching the bottom just as Tansy emerged into the hallway. The pale blue orbs took in Valery's scratched face and limbs in one quick glance, a cool, appraising glance. Before she could say anything, Tansy went on to the opposite stairway, and then Bob's figure was at the library doorway, beside Glen, looking up at Valery as she stood at the steps.

"Now this is more like it," he said. "You'll join us for dinner, of course." She liked the candidness of his frank, devouring gaze.

His directness could catch you up along with the vitality that was so encompassing. "You look perfectly lovely, especially for someone who's had the kind of morning you have," he said, taking her hand and drawing her into the library.

"I'll second that," Glen Perry said, and his gaze, softer, gentler, was rewarding in another way.

"I look better than I feel, I'm afraid," Valery said, sinking down onto the long, black-leather sofa in the paneled room. "I'm still a bit shaken, if you must know."

"A good drink will fix that," Bob exclaimed. "I'll be back with the essentials."

Valery watched him leave, Labat following him on soundless feet, shadow like, and then Glen was sitting down beside her, his eyes scanning the bookshelves, each one ending with an ornate, carved figurine.

"Very different, this place, isn't it?" he commented, his glance at her quick, affable. "How long have you been here?"

"A month ago," Valery said, "I was hired to fill in for Carlotta Van Dyne, Bob's mother, and Tansy was to have arrived a month ago. She didn't get here until today, last night sometime, to be exact."

"Then you were alone here for the past month," Glen finished.

"Except for Labat," Valery answered. "Frankly, it was getting to me. I think I'm still edgy from it."

Glen Perry's eyes were on her, casual interest in them and she noticed that he was good-looking in his quiet way. "Do you know the Van Dynes well?" he asked.

"No, I only know Carlotta Van Dyne," Valery said. "My being here is really one of those things that sometimes happens, an unexpected result of a casual meeting." Quickly she told Glen Perry how she had come to *Verdelet,* even putting in her father's displeasure over it and silently wondering why she'd felt the need to include that. "So I've never met any of the others till today," she concluded. "I'm not even sure how many more there are."

"Unless the old lady decides to come there'll just be one more, Bob's brother Martin," Glen Perry said. "Bob's told me about the family," he added quickly, answering Valery's glance. "Let's hope you've no more accidents," he said and the warmth and sincerity in his voice carried unexpected force.

"How long have you known Bob?" she questioned.

"About a year, since I joined the company," Glen said. "Bob's been with them longer. Community Planning Consultants. We're in the main office in Wayland, just outside Boston. We specialize in helping communities plan orderly growth. I guess Bob and I just sort of hit it off from the first. He's a very strong personality."

"He gets that from his mother," Valery commented.

"Talking about me?" the voice cut in, and she saw Bob, ice bucket and glasses in his hands. He extracted bottles from a cabinet in the corner and turned to her.

"What's your pleasure?" he asked.

"A manhattan would be perfect," she answered.

"One perfect manhattan coming up," he sang out. "Glen and I will have old-fashioneds. I feel like bourbon tonight, right, Glen?"

"Whatever you say, Bob," Glen Perry answered, and Valery felt herself sniff silently. Leaders and followers. Maybe that was the ideal relationship, simple, clear-cut, no inner drives, no complications of ego and pride, just acceptance and dominance.

She took the manhattan Bob handed her and took a long swallow. It was excellent, but then she'd known it would be. Bob Van Dyne wasn't the type to make anything but an excellent drink.

"To Carlotta," he said, lifting his glass and almost draining it in one long pull.

"How many of you are there exactly?" Valery asked. "Perhaps I should ask how many of you *were* there."

"Just one more besides Carlotta, Brother Martin, Tansy, and myself. That was Kenneth."

"Tansy's father?"

Bob nodded, his intense face touched, she thought, by a moment of grimness. "Though we're spread around we're actually a very close little family group. We meet a couple of times a year here. Even Labat is a distant cousin."

"I must say you've a very different way of referring to each other," Valery remarked. "You call your mother by her first name, even Tansy calls her Carlotta, and you refer to *Brother Martin*."

"We're a different kind of family," Bob grinned at her. "And Carlotta wouldn't have chosen you to take care of Tansy if she hadn't thought you would fit in right."

His grin was enveloping. "We just take a little getting used to," he added, his eyes dancing, and she found herself remembering the strongly soothing touch of his hands on her back. Suddenly she was aware of Labat's gaunt figure in the doorway, silent as a corpse, and Bob rose at once. "Dinner's ready," he sang out cheerfully, hooking his arm into hers. Glen, a puppy-dog quality to his quick smile, fell in alongside them. The big dining room where she had eaten alone for the past month had taken on a new warmth, and even the murky pictures seemed mellower. "Tansy's not joining us tonight," Bob said, pouring the wine. "She's eating in her room."

"Your idea? Punishment?" Valery questioned.

"Not really. She has some things to work out alone," he answered. She was seated beside Glen and opposite Bob and the chair at the head of the table was left unfilled. It was Carlotta Van Dyne's place, Valery guessed. Bob was a witty, entertaining dinner companion and there was no escaping the magnetism of his strong, intense personality. Anything with this man would be exciting, she told herself. Glen seemed content to stay in the background, and dinner was nearly over when Labat appeared again, his deep-socketed eyes singling out Bob though she caught his passing glance at her. The houseman still made her shudder inside, a malignant quality to the man, as though he were a human reliquary of evil.

"The phone," he said to Bob. "Brother Martin is at the village. He wants me to pick him up."

"Serve the coffee and then go get him," Bob said.

"Skip the coffee for me," Valery said. "I think I should go up and say good night to Tansy before it gets any later and she goes to sleep. I don't want to end the day with her upset at what was just an unfortunate accident, probably more my fault than hers."

"Why do you say that?" Glen questioned her, his eyes studying her intently.

"I should have realized there was probably rotted planking on that catwalk," the girl answered. "I let my annoyance at Tansy's running on out of sight get the better of me."

"All right, you go on up and talk to her," Bob interjected. "Then come back down to the library and talk to me. Glen will probably be in his room by then with a good book. He's a great one for reading in the evening."

"That's right," Glen echoed. A dismissal, casually but firmly given and quickly accepted. She glanced at Glen and found herself unaccountably annoyed at his affable smile. Bob's hand at her elbow steered her from the room, and at the foot of the stairs leading to the east wing he let his eyes hold her for a long moment. "Hurry back," he said and she knew she would ordinarily have been annoyed at the amused anticipation in his tone. Instead, she was surprised at the willing acquiescence she felt and she turned away to climb the stairs. For the first time since she had come to *Verdelet* she climbed these steps and, halfway up, feeling eyes on her, she glanced back to see that Bob had gone but Labat was there, watching her. She turned away and continued up to the second floor, laid out exactly as in the west wing except that all the rooms were on the left side of the hallway. Knocking on the door, she paused a moment and then entered the room. Tansy was seated on a bedspread of black satin with black pillows behind her. Dressed in a pale-blue nightgown, a book on her lap, she could once again have been a figurine carved there, placed against a striking backdrop, delicate, shimmering. The rest of the room was stark white, white dresser, white walls, white drapes, white table. The child lowered the book as Valery approached, the translucent blue eyes cool, haughty, unwavering. Valery felt as though she were being received by a queen.

"I came to say good night," Valery began. "I hope you're not upset about today."

Even as she said it she felt foolish. If the child was upset she hid it with magnificent aplomb. "It was just one of those things," she started again. "It wasn't anybody's fault, really. It was an accident, and accidents happen."

"Perhaps you're accident-prone," Tansy commented flatly.

"Hardly. I've had very few accidents," Valery answered, keeping down the spiral of irritation that rose inside her. "No, it just happened and, as you said, I'll have to be more careful."

She tried a broad smile, but the child remained expressionless, aloof, distant. Valery wondered whether the distant posture was a self-invoked curtain to hide behind. Distance often lent self-protection against the risk of being hurt by something said or done. It was a reasonable explanation that failed to satisfy. There was something more here, something else beyond the pale-blue eyes, and she started to turn away, trying not to sound irritated and knowing she was not being altogether successful.

"Good night, Tansy," she said. "We'll start over again tomorrow."

"Yes, we will," Tansy said, managing to infuse the three simple words with a multiplicity of shadings. Valery glanced back at the child who, she realized, had sat absolutely motionless on the black satin quilt. The Siamese cat's eyes stared back at her, telling her nothing, and she hurried out of the room, again determined to talk to Bob about the child.

He was in the library with brandies ready and she took a long sip of hers, grateful for the warmth it spread through her and glad for his very male, very animal sensuousness. There was a welcome directness to it after the frustrating impenetrability of the child.

"How'd it go?" he asked casually, sinking down beside her on the black-leather sofa.

"I don't know," Valery said from half-inside her brandy snifter. "She's a very different person, a very difficult child to reach."

"Tansy's her own master but she'll warm up," Bob said soothingly. "She's governed by people who are really strangers for so much of the time that she keeps her own privacy."

"She certainly does," Valery said. If that's all it is, she added silently. The explanation was too simple. There was more to Tansy than a mere concern for inner privacy.

"What was her father like?" she asked.

"He was the youngest of us," Bob said. "Wild, most called him. He was a Van Dyne, that's all."

It was a closed subject, she realized as he let the few words drop with a finality. There'd be no talk of the family tragedy surrounding Tansy's parents that Carlotta had mentioned in passing. She saw the dark fire in Bob's eyes, almost a hostility. He refilled her brandy snifter and she drank of it at once. She was still much too tense, she realized. The long month alone had started it and then the accident, death reaching out for her suddenly, and then the strange reaction of the child. Everything had become too intense and she leaned back, letting the brandy help. Through half-closed eyes she saw Bob watching the way her breasts pressed against her blouse. He glanced up to catch the half-smile that had touched her lips and she heard his low laugh and knew that she'd met his thoughts in mid-flight.

"I've always been told I lack subtlety," he said.

"Subtlety can be boring," she said.

"And it wastes time."

"Is time so important?"

"Always."

"You're impatient."

"That's your fault. Beauty makes for impatience."

She smiled and saw him lean toward her. Not moving, she felt her lips part, ever so slightly, all by themselves, the way a flower opens its petals at the first hint of the warm, life-giving sun. The human organism reacting to stimuli again, she reflected dimly, and then his lips were on hers, strong, gathering electricity quickly. She felt his hands on her and pressed forward to welcome them until finally, with an effort, she pulled away. "The brandy," she said, knowing it was not even a half-truth, and then he was turning her to him again. The vibrancy of the man would have made marble respond, and she was far from that. Again his lips found hers, urging, insistent, and she surprised herself by how reluctant she was to finally pull away.

"Why do you stop?" he asked. She shrugged, not sure of the answer.

"Maybe I'm not ready to not stop," she said. "I guess I just take more time."

"Then we'll hurry time," he announced. "We'll go riding tomorrow morning."

"Riding?" Valery asked. "I'm here to look after Tansy, not to go off enjoying myself."

"We'll count it as your time off for the day. Labat can see to her till we get back. Besides, it'll only be for an hour or so but it will help you to know me better."

"But I can't ride those horses. They're wild. Certainly not that big chestnut," Valery protested.

"*Vodun?* No, only I ride him."

"*Vodun.* What an interesting name. What does it mean?"

"I don't know. I heard it someplace and liked it. You'll ride *Mana.* She'll just follow along once we start."

"*Mana.* Another interesting name."

"You'll have to ask Carlotta about that one. She gave it to her. Then it's settled. We go riding in the morning."

"We'll see tomorrow. Right now I'm going upstairs and get some sleep," Valery said. Bob's arms encircled her as the sound of the front door being opened reached them.

"He's here," Bob exclaimed, stepping back. With a murmured apology he brushed past her and disappeared into the hallway. Valery heard the sound of voices and then footsteps coming toward the library. The figure that entered first came toward her on sandaled feet, trailing the gray, flowing robes of a friar, replete with the long, knotted waistcord. The face, round and full, fringed in the traditional monk's cut, would have been absolutely cherubic except for the eyes. They probed restlessly and seemed alive with an inner flame that contrasted with the soft-cheeked, round countenance.

"Hello, my dear," he said, taking Valery's hand with both of his, his voice low, mellifluous. "I'm even more sorry I couldn't get here sooner, now that I've seen you."

He turned to Bob for an instant. "Carlotta has outdone herself this time," he said, and then the moving, restless eyes were back on Valery again. "You have a look of surprise on your lovely face," he commented, and the girl nodded her head in admission.

"Now you see why I refer to *Brother* Martin," she heard Bob say.

"Then you are a brother," Valery ventured, extracting her hand from his.

"Most emphatically," he said, smiling broadly.

"Emphatically to you if not to everyone else, eh, Brother Martin?" Bob said, and Valery caught the tinge of sharpness in his voice.

"A mere detail, my dear Robert," Brother Martin said, and his smile was benign, lofty. Meanings within meanings again, Valery noted, remembering how Labat had spoken to Tansy that morning. But further wonderings were cut off as Brother Martin went on in his smooth, rich voice.

"I look forward to enjoying your company tomorrow, my dear," he said. "Now I am tired and dusty from my journeys so I shall go to my room. I'll stop in to see Tansy, first, of course. See you all tomorrow."

With a wave of his hand and a nod of the fringed head he was gone, and she felt Bob's eyes studying her.

"This is a place of surprises," she remarked.

"You'll like Brother Martin," he said. "He's a man of ideas, a philosopher." Then, reaching out quickly, he pulled her to him and his hands pressing the softly rounded sides of her breasts, kissed her hard, letting her go with equal suddenness. The moment of disappointment she felt angered her and she looked away quickly, afraid he might read it in her eyes. "Good night, again," he said and she heard the confident amusement in his voice.

"Good night," she said, turning away and forcing herself not to look back.

In her room, lying in bed, the soreness of her body returned but now there was a quiet excitement coursing through her, too. The month of aloneness and mounting nervousness had certainly ended with an explosion of activity and surprises. It was more than a little overwhelming, and suddenly she felt utterly exhausted, unable to sort out her thoughts, feeling herself drift off to sleep as a series of images floated through her mind, a huge waterwheel with an old, dead fly on it, the grisly object suddenly large, frightening. Then the other images, crowding each other, disconnected, out of sequence, lonely, gray days of utter silence and then voices, her father's voice and her own voice, arguing, rejecting, and then she was running, running, and suddenly she was falling and thick paddles bore down on her, the taste of mud and the feel of death in her mouth, and through it all the calm face of a spun-gold, shimmering little enigma. Finally the images went away and she slept soundly.

CHAPTER THREE

Valery woke with a ray of pale sun that reached into the room, edging its way across her arm, then her face. Stretching, the pain in her shoulders and back a dim reminder of the previous day, she remembered strong hands on her, rubbing, massaging. She half smiled lazily as she thought of how nice it would be to have those hands on her now, rubbing her into wakefulness, or maybe something more. She snapped off her smile, sitting up, running her hands through her cascading black hair. The thought, delicious as it was, could not be allowed room, she told herself severely. Hadn't she grown tired of giving in to the senses, of giving completely to the incomplete? That's why she'd broken with Ben Wright so coldly, knowing theirs was but a one-level attraction, and yet here she was, sensuous musings flooding over her. The hungers of the body, once wakened, were beyond stilling, she decided as she swung from the bed. The trick, of course, was not to waken them too fully in the first place. But the conclusion was one of those gratuitous insights only given us to know afterward. Nor, she smiled to herself, would she have had it any other way.

Remembering Bob Van Dyne's confident insistence, she dressed in deep blue slacks with a white shirt and a matching vest of deep blue suede. It would do for whatever the day held. When she reached the downstairs foyer, Glen was there and she saw he had on riding boots.

"Bob's in the stables, waiting for you," he smiled.

"What about Tansy?"

"He's arranged for her. Labat, I think"

"You're coming," Valery commented. "That's nice."

"No, I'm going off on my own," Glen said. "Three's a crowd, Bob reminded me."

"You always do whatever Bob wants?" Valery asked.

"More or less," Glen Perry said. His hazel eyes met hers, open, guileless. His quiet attractiveness deserved something better than he gave it, she decided. As they stepped outside she saw the gray-robed figure of Brother Martin standing alongside the terrace wall some yards away, hands behind his back, the picture of the good friar. Bob's wide grin greeted her as she rounded the corner of the stable, and he handed Glen the reins of a gray mare. She watched Glen mount and wheel the horse slowly.

"Have a good ride," Bob called to him, and he trotted off. Unaccountably annoyed, she turned to Bob.

"Do you always get what you want?" she asked. His small chuckle was rich, deep.

"Only when it's important," he grinned down at her, and she felt herself laugh with him. The big wild-eyed chestnut waited impatiently, the animal full of unreleased, driving energy, not unlike its master, she thought. A brown mare waited alongside him, and Valery was glad to see the modified English saddle with the higher cantle and small horn. Bob had gone to the big chestnut and was stroking the horse's neck soothingly. "Easy, boy, easy," she heard him say and then, with one quick motion, he was in the saddle. Valery mounted the mare, talking to her soothingly, calling her name, *Mana,* but the mare seemed docile enough and as Bob wheeled the big chestnut she followed.

"Ready?" he asked, flashing her a grin. She nodded and saw him lean forward in the saddle.

"All right, *Vodun,* go," he said to the horse and the big chestnut went off into a fast trot at once. Without urging, *Mana* followed immediately, and as they rode across the field to the right, over the rise, they circled behind the house, the big chestnut leading the way. Over the top of the ridge a field opened up in a direction she had never been. She saw the stream cutting across it and watched the big chestnut take it with ease. She'd never really jumped and she held her breath as the mare reached it but she took it cleanly, coming down easily, and Valery felt her breath released in a rush of air. "Good girl, *Mana*," she'd just said to the horse when she felt the mare break into a gallop and she looked ahead to see Bob on *Vodun*, racing full out toward a line of trees. He was a dozen yards ahead now, the trees coming up fast.

"*Mana*, whoa!" Valery called, pulling in on the reins. The mare put her head forward and increased speed. Valery yanked again on the reins with no effect. The mare was following the racing chestnut, paying no attention to the reins, probably with the bit in her teeth. The trees were just ahead and Valery saw the big chestnut plunge into them at a full gallop, not even breaking stride. She cried out as she saw Bob duck his head, thick branches brushing his hair back, and then he was racing in and out of the trees, scraping some, ducking others, clinging to the saddle as the horse flew through the woods. She pulled again on the reins, knowing it would be useless. *Mana* was following *Vodun*, into the woods at full gallop, and Valery heard her own cry of terror as the trees came at her, the horse swerving, brushing first one, then another, galloping on in a headlong rush. Valery clung to the horse's neck, pressing herself low in the saddle as thick, skull-smashing branches flashed over her head, the leaves striking against her face. Glancing on through the cluster of trees, she saw Bob look back at her, a wide grin of approval creasing his face, and then he was through the line of trees, racing into an open field. The mare swerved, cutting past a huge oak, brushing the girl's leg against the bark, raced through a narrow space beyond and, skirting a last tree, into the open.

Valery raised up in the saddle and tried the reins again but it was useless. *Mana* still chased after the wild chestnut, now some twenty-five yards ahead and widening the space between them.

Somehow, unbelievably, she was still intact, not smashed against a tree trunk or lying in the woods with a smashed skull. Ahead, Bob raced on, and suddenly she heard her gasp of horror. "No! Oh, my God, no!" she cried out as she saw the second line of trees appear ahead. She'd survived the first line but another would be certain death. Valery looked down and the ground flying past under the mare's hooves made her shrink from the thought of leaping. It would bring a broken neck probably, certainly broken bones. Looking up, she saw Bob on the chestnut racing into the second line of trees, once again at a full gallop and then, from the left, she saw the gray horse racing toward her, trying to cut her off before she reached the trees. She yanked savagely at the reins and this time the mare broke stride, only to fight back, seize the bit in her teeth again and plunge on. But the gray horse was close now and she saw Glen, low in the saddle, swing the horse in to come alongside her. The trees were less than a dozen yards away as he came alongside, reaching out to seize the mare's cheekstrap first, pulling her head to the side. As he pulled the mare in a tight circle he slipped his grip down to the rein chains at the bit, pulling down hard. The mare slowed to a snorting halt, her headlong drive broken, under control again, and Valery reined in tightly at once. As Glen's gray horse swung alongside her, she looked ahead to see Bob on the big chestnut, racing in and out of the line of trees, turning, twisting, dodging, scraping thick trunks, brushing under branches capable of sweeping him from the saddle with his head crushed in. It was an exhibition of daring, luck, practice, skilled horsemanship, and something else that defied explanation, a momumental damnation of the power of death, perhaps. Then suddenly the horse was pulled up sharply, and she watched him emerge into the open, cantering over to where she and Glen waited. She felt the tension drain from her like a vessel being emptied of its contents, and she heard the deep sound of her breath.

Bob's grin was tight, his face flushed with exhilaration, his eyes burningly bright. It was, the thought passing through her mind, as though he were a knight errant returning from a triumphal victory.

"What happened?" he asked her, eyes boring into hers, and she felt the excitement of him reach out to her. "I thought you'd rein up but when I saw you follow me through the first line of trees I assumed you'd decided to join the fun."

"Join the fun?" Valery almost choked on the words. "It was madness, that was. You could have been killed in an instant, certainly smashed into a lifelong cripple. No, I didn't decide to join you, I just couldn't stop the mare. She took off after *Vodun* and refused to stop."

His hand reached out to cover hers and his eyes turned darker, troubled, at once. "I'm sorry about that, Valery," he said, unmistakable concern in his voice. "If I'd realized that I'd have turned back to stop you myself. I didn't want you to join me. I only wanted you to watch. I thought you'd enjoy it, please believe that."

"Even watching was too much. Why do you do it, Bob?" she questioned, frowning. His laugh was loud, captivating in the animal essence of it.

"It's a fantastic experience, seeing how close you can come to death and not lose to it," he said. "It gives you a feeling of power, of overcoming the inevitable. It's really beyond description. You've got to experience it for yourself. Of course, *Vodun,* here, is like a part of me. He enjoys it, too, and we move as one."

"It's as if you were trying to kill yourself," Valery shuddered.

"Not at all," Bob laughed again. "I'm not alone in playing with death. Every auto race driver does it, every stunt flyer, every trapeze artist and high wire performer."

"You make it sound perfectly normal and natural," Valery sighed, and Bob's grin reached out to her. "Of course," he said. "Come on, we'll go back now."

He started off, leading the way, and Glen fell in alongside him while she turned the mare to catch up. The simple explanation satisfied without satisfying, flawed in ways she could not pin-point. Shaking off the thoughts she spurred the mare on and caught up with the others. Later, back at the stables, she found herself alone for a moment with Glen as they unsaddled.

"I owe you a very big thank you," she said.

"Nonsense." He smiled affably. "Glad I happened to be close enough to help." His eyes reached into hers penetratingly, as if he were considering whether to give voice to a thought, and then the moment passed and they were merely soft again, fitting his genial smile. "See you later," he said as he went off, and once again she felt herself thinking that his quiet good looks needed something better than his colorlessness.

She'd reached the house and was starting up the stairs to her room when Bob appeared, his arms encircling her waist. "I'm very upset about what happened, *Mana* running away with you, out of control that way," he said. His hand cupped her face. "I've too many plans for you to have you risk your little neck. Tansy needs you, too. Then I've some needs of my own."

The warmth of his body, steel-hard against hers, was stir-ring, and when he stepped back, letting her go, she wondered about the word need. It was not his alone, she knew. "I'm going to change," she said. "I'm afraid I worked up more excitement than I'd bargained for this morning. Tell Labat I'll take Tansy in a few minutes, please."

She hurried to her room, taking off her perspiration-soaked shirt, then the slacks, changing into a sea-green skirt and matching blouse, a very flattering color that set off the jet of her hair and the violet of her eyes. She suddenly felt like earrings and, opening the small traveling case she carried, she chose one of her favorite pairs, halfmoon drop earrings made of rose-wood and trimmed in gold, brought to her from Mozambique. Fastening on the earrings, she hurried downstairs to find a table had been set up on the terrace and Glen, Bob, and Brother Martin were there. Brother Martin's round face lighted up as she appeared, his restless eyes scanning her with a definitely un-friar-like look.

"Beautiful," he murmured. "Perfectly beautiful." He pulled a wrought-iron chair out for her. "I thought a little brunch would be in order," he said. "Besides, I love *al fresco* dining."

Valery was about to ask where Tansy was when the child appeared, holding a young cat, gray and white, hardly a year old, Valery guessed.

"Where did you find her?" Valery asked in surprise.

"Found her back of the house," Tansy replied, settling herself into one of the chairs with the cat on her lap. "Now you stay there, cat," Tansy said. She wore a blue denim coverall over a black jersey turtle neck shirt and her long, shimmering hair fell perfectly to frame her face. She would keep her porcelain beauty no matter what she wore, Valery thought, watching the child stroke the cat with long hand motions that were almost machine like in their fluidity. Labat appeared with biscuits, ham and cheese, and hot tea, and Valery realized she was hungry. Brother Martin had taken the chair beside her, his portly form filling it, letting the loose gray robes spill outward.

"I love your earrings, my dear," he commented. "They're from the Mediterranean basin, I'll wager, Africa, perhaps?"

"Mozambique," Valery answered in between biscuits. "I've never seen any quite like them."

"I hear you were upset by Robert's little game this morning," he chuckled, the round face beaming at her.

"I'm afraid so," she admitted. "Bob explained it so it all sounded quite ordinary but I'm afraid I still don't understand it that way, race car drivers, trapeze artists, and the like notwithstanding. What he was doing seemed somehow different from those things."

"A more direct confrontation, that's all," Brother Martin beamed. "It was merely my brother's way of affirming his allegiance to a principle."

"A principle?" Valery echoed.

"Yes, the principle that death, the end, the great finality is what makes life interesting. Death is not something to be afraid of. It is a fascinating, beautiful thing of infinite variety. Think, life comes to us in only one way but death can come in a thousand different ways. I have always been fascinated by the finalities that surround death, which is of course a finality of itself. But man alone has been given the ability to make a conscious decision about death. The lesser creatures know death only as an end-product of the food-gathering process. Man, however, knows death as part of the pattern of existence. But to most of us, the beginning governs the end. A child well-raised will come to a good end and an imprudent life will be a short one. Unfortunately, it is the other way around. The end governs all that comes before it, whether we are aware of it or not. When we examine the last things of life, the finalities, as it were, we begin to realize how true that is. Our actions are made clear for us in any situation. No matter what it is, when we examine the end, we know what we must do as if it had been preordained. Death is the ultimate of all finalities, of course, and the total governor of all our acts. Its infinite variety has always fascinated me but I am most fascinated by the relation of death to living man. Man can use death in so many ways. It's really all a matter of realizing that death is only another finality, another last thing, and that the last things are the most important things in whatever we do."

"That highly individual view is only one of Brother Martin's profound observations," Bob cut in, and Valery glanced up to see his grin was tight, little lines of strain at the corners of his mouth. "That's why Brother Martin's vocation has been a strictly personal one for some years, now, a Brotherhood of one," he went on, and Valery heard the mockery in his voice. His words wheeled around in her mind, and her eyes, questioning, half-formed thoughts in their violet depths, looked at Brother Martin. His smile was lofty.

"That is Robert's way of telling you that the Order and I parted company some years ago," he said.

"I see." Valery frowned. "At least I think I do." She glanced at Tansy and saw the child methodically stroking the cat. Glen's face was hopelessly bland and then she glanced at Bob to see him watching her, the tight grin still fixed on his face. She turned back to Brother Martin.

"Then you're not really a Brother, now," she said. She groped for words, feeling tongue-tied and stupid. "You were..."

"Defrocked?" Brother Martin offered. "Certainly not. As you can see, I'm very much frocked."

His chuckle was soft, private. "Besides, they don't defrock Brothers. I was *separated* from the Order. As it was their idea entirely, I do not consider myself as anything else but a Brother. They decided that I was, in their words, obsessed with the eschatological view of life."

He paused, flashed a cherubic smile at Valery, and clapped his hands together. "But this is all too, too deep for this time of day," he said. "It's what I call evening talk. The night lends substance to talk of deep and mysterious things, don't you think, my dear?"

Valery didn't bother to try to answer as he went on without waiting. "Perhaps tonight, after dinner, we can pursue it further."

He stood up abruptly, almost imperiously, his gray robes swirling around him. The movement startled the cat, and Valery saw the animal leap from Tansy's lap in one lithe bound, landing on the terrace to stand there as if frozen in one spot, her back slightly arched. Taking a last sip of tea, still mentally digesting Brother Martin's words, she saw Tansy get up and reach for the cat.

"Here cat," Tansy called. The cat moved away a few steps.

"Here, I'll pet you some more," Tansy said, moving after the cat. The cat retreated again, leaning to one side, uncertain, suddenly, of her place here.

"Come here, cat," Tansy said. Valery heard the child's tone suddenly grow sharp, demanding. The cat stepped back and Valery saw her back arch.

"Damn, cat, come here, I said," Tansy shot out and at the same instant, sprang forward to grab the cat. Valery saw the animal's paw lash back in instinctive reaction, a movement almost too swift to catch. Tansy halted, her arm still extended, the cat still drawn away from it, the scene as a still photo caught by a passing cameraman. A thin red line of blood bubbled almost magically on the back of Tansy's hand and the child stared at it for a long moment. When she looked up, it was as though she had been suddenly drenched in ice and Valery felt the small shudder of her body.

Tansy's translucent blue eyes held pinpoints of cold fury. Valery glanced away to see Bob and Brother Martin both watching the child intently, and when she looked back at Tansy the pale-blue eyes were expressionless once again. It had all been so brief, so passing, that she wasn't sure she hadn't seen things that weren't really there.

"Cats will be cats," she heard Glen say.

"Yes, they're so like people," Brother Martin observed, and Valery shot a glance at him but he didn't amplify the remark. She rose and went over to Tansy, taking the child's hand.

"A Band-Aid will cover that. I've some with my things," she said. "I'll get one." She hurried off, glad for the few moments alone. The Van Dynes were an overwhelming family, each in a highly individual way, she decided, each so very different from the others and yet there was a thread that ran through them, a theme that linked them together, an unusual concern with death. Tansy and her fascination with an old dead fly, an old abandoned mill; Brother Martin with his views on the finalities of things; even Bob had it with his headlong galloping through the woods, "a direct confrontation," Brother Martin had called it. She got the Band-Aid from her bathroom and hurried back down to the terrace, thinking about Brother Martin, the ex-brother, clothed in friar's robes outside and heaven knows what inside. But, as it seemed the others called him Brother Martin, she would also, she concluded.

The terrace was empty except for Glen and Tansy she saw in some surprise.

"Bob said he'd see you later," Glen volunteered. "He and Brother Martin had family business to go over."

"I want to go down to the lake and hunt frogs," Tansy said firmly, and Valery saw that she had hold of the cat again in a firm grip.

"Frogs? I never saw anything but dragonflies, water beetles, and mosquitoes there," Valery said. "No, come to think of it, I did see a tadpole once," she added, remembering the moment of silent, savage death she'd witnessed. "So perhaps there are frogs down there."

"There are frogs, live ones, and dead ones that float upside down. They're the most fun to watch," Tansy said.

Valery glanced quickly at the child but Tansy's opaque-blue eyes were unrevealing, sphinx-like. But it was there again, the affinity for death.

"We're taking cat along," Tansy said.

"See that she doesn't scratch you again," Valery cautioned, and Tansy's smile was the quick, mask like one she had seen before.

"She won't," the child said, and Valery wondered if she imagined a certain grimness undercoating the sweet simplicity of the reply.

"The lake it is then," Valery said, starting after the long blond hair in the blue denims, pausing a moment in front of Glen.

"Thanks again for this morning," she said.

His smile was affable. "No more accidents today," he said, and his hazel eyes held a seriousness in them that didn't fit the bland smile. Or was she imagining again? Imagining came easily here at this place of contrasts and surprises, she had already concluded.

"No more accidents," she laughed and hurried on to catch up with Tansy. The child walked with brisk purposefulness, holding the cat securely cradled in her arms, making no attempt at conversation. She would, Valery knew, have to find a way to communicate with the child. But words, mere conversation, would not do it, not with this haughty, withdrawn child. But do we ever really communicate with words, she reflected. Certainly she and her father found words easy but communication almost impossible. No, not words, they could be nothing more than so many little masks or so many little daggers. Reaching out, that was communication, reaching out without pretenses or postures, and that was the hard thing. It was hard now, even with the child, Valery admitted to herself, aware of her own irritation with Tansy. She didn't like puzzles, riddles, unfathomable things, and Tansy certainly fitted in that catagory.

As they crested the rise and started down to the lake, Valery cast a glance behind her at the house. It hugged the ground, squatting there like a corpulent old hag, defiantly overdressed, wearing its excesses proudly. There was almost a carnality to the house that could possess one's imagination. In just the one month she'd lived there she had felt it. To live and grow up in it could certainly color the soul, she reflected, its overwrought, overripe turbulence investing all within its walls. Each, of course, would have been affected in his or her way: Brother Martin and his obsessions; Kenneth, the slain one and his wildness; and Bob and his tremendous vibrancy. Even Carlotta Van Dyne had no doubt taken of it, Valery mused, the old dowager's imperiousness having doubtlessly been towering in former years. Only Tansy stood alone, seeming to have escaped the excesses that came from *Verdelet*, a part of the heritage of the place. Instead of turbulent, she was sphinx-like. Instead of fire, she was ice. Instead of grossness, she was glacial purity. She seemed out of place here at *Verdelet*.

They reached the lake's unruffled, sun-burnished surface and Tansy halted at the soft grass beside the shore. Holding the cat with one hand, she pointed with the other to a stretch of tall grass, reeds, and cattails.

"I'm going there, into the reeds. You can watch me from here," she announced.

"Why can't I come with you?" Valery questioned, more out of curiosity than desire. Tramping through the waist-high reeds was hardly inviting.

"You'll interfere with my frog-hunting. It requires careful silence," Tansy said. "See that flat rock beyond the reeds, the one with the tree that hangs over it? I won't go beyond there."

Valery took in the rock that projected into the lake and the overhanging tree, both clearly visible.

"All right, but no further, remember," she agreed. Tansy flashed the brief, mirthless smile and moved away, still holding the cat. Sinking down on the grass, grateful for the sun's rare appearance, she watched the spun-gold hair appear and disappear among the reeds at the water's edge. The child would pause, then go on, lost from sight for long stretches, only to reappear again. Sinking back on the grass, Valery found she could have slept if she hadn't felt the need to watch the child. As it was she half dozed, snapping awake every few minutes to sit up and scan the reeds for the blond head. Once, when the glint of gold hair didn't appear, she got to her feet and called out and the head bobbed up from the tall grasses a few yards out from the shore. But the warm sun withdrew when the afternoon was half over, and a wind, sharp and chilling, came to poke and prod. Looking at her watch, Valery suddenly thought of Fred Wheaten. In little less than an hour he'd be at the glen. Of course, he'd no doubt been there yesterday and when she hadn't come had realized Tansy had arrived. He'd probably heard as much anyway. News travels in its own ways in these hamlets, she had learned long ago. But he'd go to the glen anyway, hoping she might make it for a last lesson or two. That was the character of the man and she decided to go to meet him there if she could. It was the proper thing to do and she owed him a debt of gratitude, she reflected, remembering all the lonely days.

"Tansy!" she called but the child's back was to her and she felt the wind whip her cry away. She called again and saw it was useless from this distance. "Damn!" she muttered as she started through the reeds and tall grasses. The footing was very uneven and she stumbled, half fell, caught herself and went on only to stumble again and then again. Halfway to the rock she turned her ankle and fell, disappearing into the reeds. Pulling herself up, she rubbed her ankle for a moment and then called to Tansy again. This time her voice reached and she saw the child turn to look at her, the round, opaque eyes expressionless as usual.

"It's time to go back," Valery called. "It's getting too chilly to stay without a sweater."

She saw Tansy's shrug, faint condescension in the gesture, and the child stepped from the rock to come toward her, hardly taller than the reeds.

"Where's the cat?" Valery asked as they started to push their way back through the tall grass.

"She ran away. I put her down and she ran away," Tansy replied.

"Shouldn't we look for her and bring her back to the house?" Valery questioned.

"No," Tansy said, making the one word absolute and final. Valery saw the blue orbs turn full on her. "She'll return to wherever she came from," Tansy added.

This time it was Valery's turn to shrug and she did so as she walked behind Tansy, trying to stumble as few times as possible. The uneven footing didn't seem to bother the child at all, Valery saw, and when she reached the end of the reeds Tansy was waiting for her, the cool eyes tinted with boredom. A lacewing brushed her face and the eyes remained impassive. The insect darted away and Valery felt it against her cheek. She put a hand up to brush it away and immediately felt the emptiness at her ear. "My earring!" she exclaimed. "I've lost it." Quickly touching her other ear, she felt the smoothness of the half-moon securely in place. "I must have lost it one of the times I stumbled. I'm going back to see if I can find it."

"You won't find it, not in all those reeds and the tall grass," Tansy said. The child's lofty tone irritated.

"I lost an earring on a picnic once and found it," Valery snapped. "I just might do it again. You can wait here or you can come help me look."

"I'll go on to the house," Tansy said coldly.

"No, I'll take you and then come back," Valery answered brusquely. She marched the child to the house in silence and found Glen on the terrace with a book.

"Bob went to town," he called to her. "Brother Martin's inside somewhere. How was the lake today?"

"I lost an earring and I'm going back to look for it," Valery said.

"Want some help?" Glen asked. Tansy's voice, coldly commanding, cut off Valery's answer.

"Play some lawn tennis again with me," the child said to Glen, and Valery caught Glen's quick look of surprise and hesitation.

"Stay with Tansy," she said quickly. "I'll find it if it's to be found."

Hurrying off, she realized she was angry at the combination of things, an inner tension that still clung to her, her stupidity in not taking off the earrings before starting through the reeds, her inability to reach through Tansy's icy shield. Cresting the rise, she hurried on to the lake, pulling off the other earring and thrusting it into the pocket of her skirt. The chill wind that had blown up was still there and it rifled through her hair. Yet the reeds hardly moved, standing silent as pallbearers. She pushed through them, retracing her steps as best she could, head lowered, eyes scanning the ground for a glimpse of gold trim on wood. Pushing aside tall grass, moving the thicker reeds with both hands, she suddenly reflected that the quiet caution of her search was ridiculous. If she found it at all it would be pure luck and nothing else and recklessly, angrily, she swept aside the reeds, sweeping each area that opened up before her with her glance. Finally, glancing up, she saw she was almost at the flat rock with the overhanging tree, past where she had halted to call Tansy. Grimacing, she turned and started back again, moving six inches to the left to trace a new path back. She had gone but a few yards when, pushing aside a thick clump of reeds, the small gray-white object caught her eye. Pressing the reeds further aside, she peered down at it and heard her shocked gasp. It was the cat, lying silent and still on its side. Kneeling down, she felt the involuntary shudder go through her body. The cat's head was grotesquely twisted away from its body, its neck broken.

Shrinking back, the girl rose, the gruesome find making her stomach tighten, and she watched the reeds snap back in place to hide the still, lifeless form. She turned, shaken, surprise and disgust mingling with something unformed and nameless, and she hurried away, forcing herself not to run. An animal had killed the cat, of course, she said silently, and found herself unwilling to accept the explanation. But that had to be the explanation, she told herself, shaking away the questions that instantly crowded in on her. An animal, she repeated, one strong enough and large enough to seize the cat's neck and twist it or shake it into breaking. Half-running now, she reached the edge of the reeds and pushed through the last of them, pausing for breath. How appropriate, she frowned, that they should stand so unmoving in deathlike stillness. The sight of the cat stayed with her as she hurried along the path back toward the house. She'd not thought of the earring since coming on the grisly discovery and now, as she neared the house, she saw Glen and Tansy to the left playing tennis on the grass. Bob's broad-shouldered form was there, watching them and, as he turned at her approach she saw the round, robed figure of Brother Martin behind him. She heard Glen's voice as, without pausing in his play, he called out to her.

"Find the earring?" he asked.

"No earring," she answered, hearing the grimness in her voice, looking up to see Bob's deep eyes studying her intently.

"What's the matter?" he questioned. "You look a little shaken."

"I guess so," she replied quietly. "I found the cat." She glanced at Tansy and Glen and saw the game halt at once, Tansy's round eyes fully on her, waiting, and Valery hesitated, suddenly afraid of shocking the child.

"You didn't bring her back, I see," Tansy said slowly.

"No," Valery said, deciding to plunge on. "She was dead. Her neck was broken."

The moment of stillness was short, broken by Tansy's calm, disdainful voice.

"It served her right," she said.

"*Tansy!*" Valery exploded the word. "You can't mean that." Staring at the round, opaque blue orbs she saw the icy coldness of them.

"You saw her scratch me," Tansy said. "I reached out to her and she scratched me."

"But that was just an instinctive reaction on the cat's part," Valery said incredulously.

"I reached out to her and she scratched me," Tansy repeated. There was no doggedness, Valery saw, no stubborn truculence, only a chilling hauteur.

"And for that she deserved to be killed?" Valery exclaimed, hearing the disbelief in her voice. Valery held the child's unwavering stare, trying to see behind the twin blue masks of her eyes. Tansy's disdainful shrug was frighteningly adamant. Brother Martin's voice intruded, softly insistent.

"Valery, my dear, I think I can explain what Tansy means," the girl heard him say and she turned to him, her frown deep. Brother Martin's smile was calm, placating in his cherubic face.

"Tansy merely means that those who reject are killers themselves, deserving of what they have done," he said. Valery felt the surge of instant resentment inside herself.

"That's ridiculous," she threw back angrily. "How can you even say a thing like that?"

"Because it's true," the soft-cheeked face smiled at her. "Those who reject are killers. Perhaps they don't physically kill someone when they reject but they kill. They kill kindness, they kill hope, they kill love. That alone could be considered deserving of death, don't you agree?"

"No, I don't agree," Valery snapped, furious at the whirling mixture of feelings inside herself, feelings that were quick to sort themselves out in uncomfortable proportions.

"You're upset, my dear," Brother Martin said. "I'm afraid your unpleasant discovery has shaken you."

"I guess so," Valery glared. "I certainly don't think the poor little thing deserved any punishment, to say nothing of being killed." She watched Brother Martin's smile remain. His small shrug was so much like Tansy's.

"Death, my dear, is a part of all nature and all living things, indigenous to life, you might say," he commented. "In this case, a raccoon probably, or perhaps a possum or a muskrat."

"I've never seen an animal at the lake, or anywhere in this hollow for that matter," Valery said.

"Nevertheless they are there," Brother Martin said. "And now you've evidence of their existence with your own eyes."

"Yes, with my own eyes," Valery said, turning away, her stomach churning, suddenly realizing that she'd found that resentment and guilt were secret companions. Her eyes swept the others—Bob's handsome face clouded with concern as he watched her, Tansy's icy stare, Glen's expression irritating in its mildness—and she knew suddenly she had to get away alone. No, she corrected herself, not alone, to talk to Fred Wheaten, someone apart from *Verdelet* and the Van Dynes. Unformed, unsorted questions tumbled about like so many weightless space-riders in her mind. Maybe Fred Wheaten could help answer some, maybe he couldn't. She had to try, anyway.

"I'm going for a walk," she said, turning away and finding Bob at her side, his hand on her arm.

"How about company?" he asked quietly, his smile tight, his eyes deep. She shook her head, holding to her decision.

"I understand," he said. She let her gratitude color her eyes for a long moment, and then she hurried off. Walking quickly, she went down the road, conscious of the others watching her, even Labat standing to one side by the stables. Finally she passed beyond their sight over the rise and hurried down the road toward town, casting a glance at the sky that was quickly bringing night to the land. She hoped Fred Wheaten would still be waiting, and at the trio of silver birches she turned and made her way through them into the little glen. The square figure on the log rose as she entered, a happy smile wreathing the genial face.

"I almost didn't wait," he said. "I figured you were busy again."

"I managed to get away," Valery said. "Sorry I couldn't make it yesterday. You know, of course, that the Van Dynes arrived, all except Carlotta, that is. Maybe descended would be a better word."

"Yes, I heard but I hoped you could get away for one last session. Just one. It's kind of late today to start, though. Maybe you could make it once more tomorrow?"

"Maybe. I'll try, though I can't promise. But I want to ask you something, Fred. You're friendly with just about everyone. I know that the people in town don't want anything to do with the Van Dynes or the house. Do you know why? I'd like to know more if you can tell me anything, especially about Tansy."

"In town they think the place is cursed," Fred Wheaten said simply.

"*Cursed!* But why?" Valery asked.

"There've been so many tragedies connected with it and the Van Dynes. I don't believe in talk about anything being cursed but some places and some families do seem to have more than their share of trouble and bad luck."

"Yes, that's true. And that's how it's been at *Verdelet?*"

Fred Wheaten shook his head solemnly. "Only a year ago there was Aran Tenner," he began. "He was a stableman, hired and brought up from North Carolina. He wound up killing Marie Ridove, a girl from New Brunswick, in a fit of raging jealousy. Before that there were the Boltons, a young couple they'd hired to look after Tansy. She killed her husband in a quarrel. Some say she'd grown sweet on young Bob Van Dyne but that could've been just talk. Anyway, the poor thing's been in an asylum ever since, her mind completely gone. And of course, there was the incident with the child and her friend from town."

"Tansy?"

"Yes, she must have been about nine, then. She and a little girl from the village used to play together. One afternoon, it seems, they went to that lake on the Van Dyne property. Many of the trees grow right down to the water. There's one that extends over a long, flat rock."

"Yes, I think I know the one."

"Well, according to the story the Van Dyne child told later, they'd gone climbing trees that afternoon. The Van Dyne child said she grew tired but the other little girl wanted to climb some more on the tree over the rock. They argued and Tansy went home. The girl from town was found in the lake that night when they went searching for her, drowned, of course."

"She'd fallen out of the tree into the lake," Valery finished.

"Yes, and apparently she'd hit the edge of that flat rock or a submerged one. Her neck was broken," Fred Wheaten added. "And there've been other things, too."

"That's enough, Fred. I've heard enough," Valery said quickly, feeling suddenly sick, a knot in the pit of her stomach, a small gray-white object amid the reeds moving through her mind in ghostly stillness. She rose and started from the glen, hearing Fred Wheaten's voice as though it were coming from a great distance. "Can you make it tomorrow?" he was asking, and she heard her own reply, given without looking back. "I'll see," she said. "I'll try."

She hurried, wanting to be alone, once again pushing back the thoughts that crowded in on her, trying to suspend the action of her mind. She concentrated on hurrying down through the near-dark pathway toward the house and then, when it came in sight, on the grossness of it. The lower windows were lighted, and she saw the lights on the second floor. She tried to pick out Tansy's room. Reaching the door, she slipped inside quietly, glad no one was in the hallway, and hurried up the stairs to her room. She turned the lamp on at once and sank down onto the bed, wishing the knot in her stomach would stop tightening. Lying back on the bed, she stretched out, stayed for hardly a long minute and then rose to walk to the window and then back to the bed again, pacing restlessly, her entire body seething, her thoughts pounding insistently. Thoughts, she grimaced as she returned to the window, creditors of the mind, refusing to be ignored. Payment, they demanded, and payment was to be recognized, given admittance, welcome or unwelcome. Nothing less would do, she realized, and she returned to the bed to sink down on it again, at once ashamed of what terrible things the mind can harbor. Tansy! The name rolled across her mind. Tansy and the grotesquely twisted neck of the cat. Valery shuddered. The cat's neck broken and the little girl from town who'd drowned in the lake with her neck broken. Coincidence and nothing more, she told herself. To think that Tansy could have killed the cat was of itself sickening. To think anything more was shattering. Yet the images stayed, clinging to her consciousness. They paraded across her mind, sorting themselves out with unnerving clarity. Tansy's perfect little face floated in front of her, and she saw the pinpoints of fury in those translucent eyes as the cat scratched her. Maybe she hadn't imagined them at all. Tansy had been insistent on taking the cat to the lake with them and once again the lifeless form of the animal was in her mind, no blood on it, no signs of another animal's bite, just the twisted, broken neck, and then she heard a voice, Tansy's voice, and the chilling satisfaction in it: *it served her right.*

Valery felt her skin quiver. The pieces were there. They formed a picture, if the picture could be believed. And if so, what then? If Tansy had indeed killed the cat, twisted its neck till it broke, what of the little girl from town? Valery heard her own gasp whispered in the silence of the room. *"No!"* The thought was its own Pandora's box of horror. Certainly there'd been an investigation at the time and everything was found in order. But then, she reflected, there had really been nothing to investigate. There'd only been Tansy's story of what had happened. The tragedy had been pieced together from that and the only reasonable conclusion reached. It was simple as that, Valery told herself angrily. She had no right to the thoughts that kept floating through her mind. She was being as overwrought as this excessive house. Damn, why wouldn't the sight of the cat's twisted neck go away? The one didn't have to connect with the other.

Tansy could be cold steel, Valery reminded herself. She'd learned that as she lay on the mudbank outside the old mill. The child's reactions were twisted, the result of some inner psychic warping, and she probably could be cruel beyond the cruelty inherent in most children. Perhaps she had killed the cat. The thought was horrible enough by itself. To carry it further was to enter a terrible world, to intimate that under that fragile, spun-gold beauty there was a monster. The thought was too horrible and Valery flung it aside. But even as she did so she saw the thin, porcelain-beauty form of the child standing on the flat rock beneath the overhanging tree, too absorbed to hear her call. Why had Tansy gone to that rock to stand beneath the tree from which the little girl from town had fallen into the lake? The question vibrated insistently. Was it because Tansy had killed the cat? That affinity for death again? Or was there another connection?

Valery pressed her palms into her face, rubbing the thought from her mind again. She felt dirty, ashamed of herself again. She'd no right to such thoughts. The picture was not that clear. The pattern too fraught with unanswered and unanswerable questions and she quickly summoned up the comfort of logic. Tansy's twisted reactions, her impenetrable wall, could simply be the result of the Van Dyne history of tragic incidents, that and the results of Brother Martin's thinking. Valery felt the instantaneous flood of resentment at the man's philosophy of life. Rejection and killing, he had said, linking them together, all part of one thing. Of course, he was ridiculously wrong, Valery grimaced, angry at how the very idea upset her. It was one of those insidious theories that always found its own spot to take root, she decided, a philosophical weed.

"Damn!" she said sharply, aloud, as suddenly she was seeing her father's face before her. What would his well-ordered mind make of all this, she wondered, and she felt a rush of warmth as she thought of him, surprising herself by the intensity of it. She turned away at once from the question, glancing at her watch, seeing it was nearly time for dinner. No more questions now, she told herself severely. Certainly not about herself. There were enough questions of their own here at *Verdelet.*

Taking the earring from her pocket, she paused, wondering whether to throw it away, and then she placed it in her small jewelry box that sat atop the dresser. Maybe the other one would turn up, a lucky chance. One could always hope. She changed into a pale-lavender dress with a low neck, edged with white piping around the collar, brushed her onyx hair quickly, and hurried from the room.

CHAPTER FOUR

Valery had hardly crossed the threshhold of the dining room when Bob was at her side, his hand warm, strong, on her arm. "I was about to come up and see what was keeping you," he said, guiding her to the chair beside his at the table. Tansy sat across from her, between Glen and Brother Martin, for whom, with his robes, the candlelight was particularly appropriate. Labat, for all his gaunt bulk, moved ghostlike on silent steps as he served.

"You look lovely," Bob whispered in a voice that everyone heard.

"I second that," Brother Martin added.

Glen's smile was quick, shy, and in the candlelight his face seemed to take on strength, a quiet steadiness. How deceiving candlelight could be, she murmured to herself.

"I'm glad you've gotten over being so upset, my dear."

It was Brother Martin's voice intruding on her thoughts, and she turned to smile at him. "My walk helped," she said. It was a half-truth, anyway, she reflected.

"Long walks always help," Brother Martin went on. "Of course, not like buying a new hat. They say nothing lifts a woman's spirits faster than that."

"Or getting an unexpected compliment," Bob added.

"Or meeting her secret lover."

Tansy's clear, quiet voice offered the last comment, and Valery felt her hands tighten as she glanced at the child. Tansy's small, enigmatic smile stayed fixed.

"What do you know about the pleasures of secret lovers, young lady?" Brother Martin asked. "Nothing but girl talk at school, I'll wager," he added.

Tansy's smile took on a secret wisdom. "Secret meetings, secret lovers," she said. "I know about a lot of things." Her eyes, bland, expressionless, touched Valery for a moment and the girl felt the chill sweep through her. Was it all only the bragging of a precocious child, idle commentary? Or something more?

Valery took a sip of wine, letting the glass hide her grimace. The child couldn't have followed her. She'd left them all on the lawn and would have been aware of anyone coming after her. *Labat!* The man's gaunt figure passed along the other side of the table from her. He could have seen her go into the glen to meet Fred Wheaten during the weeks she'd waited here alone. Perhaps Tansy's remarks had been just so much empty talk. Without knowing more she would remain silent, she decided quickly. A sudden rush of hurried explanations now would be, at best, awkward and difficult to make sound believable. She'd find a way to get to the glen and meet Fred tomorrow and insist he tell Frances at once. He'd agree, of course, she knew. That way, if tongues had somehow started wagging they could wag for nothing. She put down her wine glass, making certain her face was as cooly composed as Tansy's was bland.

"Children mature so much more quickly these days, it seems," Brother Martin commented.

"Some children," Valery said, more quickly than she had intended.

"I think that's all for the better," the round, fringe-topped face smiled at her. "They learn that much sooner how little we know about our own natures. They learn quickly that we grope and flounder about in our own little whirlpools and that we're not at all governed by goodness and love."

"You don't believe in the power of love, as a force for good?" Valery questioned.

"We don't understand what we should love because we don't want to recognize our own natures," Brother Martin answered. "We tell ourselves we want to do what's right when we really don't want that at all. We want to do what's best for ourselves and nothing else. I think people are fascinating when the self-imposed restraints of right and wrong and social morality are set aside. Then we see the real nature of man."

"You're saying the human condition is sinful, evil, selfish," Valery said. "That's been said before. Even if that's so there are other things that guide us, a power beyond ourselves. Don't tell me with your background you don't believe that."

"The good shepherd guiding our steps, eh?" The round, cherubic face leaned forward, the restless eyes bright, intent.

"Yes, that's as good a term as any," Valery threw back. "We are guided to be better than we are. Our restraints are not just self-imposed. Our impulses are not all selfish. There is a part of us that listens to the command to do the right thing, the good thing. If evil is a part of us, so is good. If we can hate, we can love."

"But it's such an uneven contest," Brother Martin chided. "The good shepherd is truly a voice crying in the wilderness, hardly a match for the others."

"The others?" Valery frowned.

"Yes, the other shepherds, my dear, all the dark shepherds of the soul. They are the ones who shepherd our lusts, our desires, our real selves. All the dark shepherds of the soul. You know them, we all know them. We like to delude ourselves that they don't exist but they do. Strangely enough, medieval man didn't have that problem of self-delusion. Perhaps medieval man was closer to the basics of existence, the unvarnished, unsophisticated urges of the human condition, but he recognized that the deep, dark parts of our natures were not merely textbook theories. They knew them then as a part of man. Peter Breughel the Elder, Hieronymus Bosch, they chronicled them in their paintings and engravings, gluttony, greed, hate, selfishness, sloth, all the others they could set forth graphically. Have you ever seen their works, my dear?"

Valery nodded distastefully, recalling works that seemed determined to test the beholder's ability to withstand their unrelieved repulsiveness.

"And even they avoided depicting the deepest urges of the human psyche, the urge to destroy, to kill, to hurt. These are as basic to us as sleep and hunger. We've called them evil urges but they are perfectly normal and natural," Brother Martin went on.

"I can't believe that," Valery cut in.

"Of course, you can, if you're honest with yourself," the round face answered, the restless eyes glittering. "Once you've wanted to hurt, once you've struck at someone in one way or another and felt the pleasure of it, you know how true my words are."

"No, I don't admit that," Valery said, hearing her voice carrying an edge of stridency. "We've all struck at someone sometime or another and very often it's been justified. Even then we don't necessarily enjoy it."

"But we do enjoy it. It's wonderful. It makes us feel strong, powerful. We merely resist admitting that to ourselves, just as you do. But we've all tasted of those ferine pleasures. The rest is merely a matter of degree. Give us enough motive, enough provocation, and we will go as far down the paths of darkness and depravity as we need go. Given the chance, the dark shepherds of our soul will lead us. They will see to it that their work is successful."

"And good, the force of love and right, the good shepherd, all that is helpless? I think you're the one who underestimates man's nature."

"No, no, my dear. It's simply a matter of recognizing obligations. We have all given the dark shepherds little bits and pieces of our souls. We have let them file their claims on us, and they need only wait for the right moment and the right place to fulfill their stewardship. They know what the finality will be. The eschatological approach again, I'm afraid."

Valery felt her cheeks hot, heard herself almost stammering and her fury at herself making it worse.

"I haven't given away little bits and pieces of myself," she said. "They have no claims on me."

"Haven't you?" Brother Martin's eyes turned fully on her, a tint of amusement just behind their surface agreeableness. "Then you are most fortunate, aren't you? And a rare person indeed."

The knot of anger Valery felt was directed at the complacent certainty of the man, she assured herself. Only that and the thought of how his ideas could affect Tansy. No wonder the child held to such strange attitudes and complexes. She heard Bob's voice break in.

"This has been entirely too serious," he was saying. "You've hardly touched your food, Valery," he chided.

"I'm not hungry tonight," the girl said. Tansy, she noted, had eaten extremely well.

"I'm afraid I've taken up all of dinner with such heavy subjects that now you have to try and make up for it, Bob," Brother Martin said, and Valery glanced at Bob to see his infectious grin directed at her.

"A situation exactly to my liking," he said in mock seriousness. "A challenge for me."

She felt his hand at her elbow, lifting her as he rose. "A nice walk in the night air is my first prescription," he said.

"I'll get a sweater," she answered, welcoming the chance to get away from the house, from Brother Martin, feeling once again the overwhelmingness of the Van Dynes. All except Bob. His kind of overwhelmingness was something else. "I'm going to my room," Tansy said. Valery met the luminous eyes boring into her, a masked meaning swimming in them. Turning, she hurried up the stairs, reminding herself of Tansy's remarks about secret lovers. Seeing Fred tomorrow was a priority item, she vowed again. Taking a lightweight, gray cardigan from the closet she hurried back down the stairs to find Bob and Glen in the hallway.

"How about you playing Brother Martin a game of chess," Bob tossed off casually as he steered Valery toward the door. "There's a nice set in the library."

She saw the docile acceptance in Glen's face and glanced quickly up at Bob, suddenly irritated, unsure which bothered her most, Glen's docility or Bob's arrogant dominance. The latter, she decided, was at least positive. Not terribly admirable perhaps but at least positive. Bob linked his arm in hers, pulling her close to him as they went into the night. He walked up from the house, along a line of rhododendron bushes and into a cluster of young saplings. A low moon filtered through the widely spaced trees and the night air smelled faintly of honeysuckle. Bob's vibrancy curled itself around her, dissipating Brother Martin's words until he brought them to the fore again.

"You mustn't mind Brother Martin," he said. "He can get to one, though, can't he?"

"Not really," she said, and wondered if she were lying convincingly. "Not to me, anyway. But I wonder how much influence his ideas have had on Tansy. His thoughts about those who reject being killers in one way or another."

Valery paused and Bob's eyes peered at her intently, watching her moment of hesitation. "Go on," he said quietly.

"All right," she said, taking a deep breath. "It makes me wonder about the cat."

"What about the cat?" Bob's voice was soft, flat.

"Whether she did kill it?" Valery blurted out, her distaste at the thought tinting each word.

"Why do you think she might have?"

"It would have been carrying through some of those ideas of Brother Martin's."

"No other reason?"

The question was casual but edged and she was glad for the darkness that hid the tenseness of her jaw.

"No other reason," she said, backing away from the subject in haste. To say now that she knew about the tragedy of the little girl from town would almost be an implied accusation, something she'd no wish to make, nor even to think about. She saw Bob's smile slowly move across his face, a knowing, contained smile, and she wondered if she hadn't said too much already. Not hurting seemed suddenly a lot more important than it used to be.

"We've seen quite a bit of human behavior here in these parts," he said. "Brother Martin's ideas may not be all that wrong."

Valery started to shake her head when Bob's hand stopped her, holding her chin, his deep eyes glistening with a dark fire even in the night. "No more," he said with soft sternness. "I didn't bring you out here for more of that kind of talk. I'd something much better in mind."

She saw his face bend toward her, heard his whispered words "Like this," and then his lips were parting hers, hungry, electric, and at once she felt the urgent, animal sensuousness of the man and once again it was compelling in its uncomplicated, forceful purity. She opened her lips to him, felt his hands, strongly sensitive, moving down across her shoulders, pausing to caress the skin of her collarline and then move down to cup her breasts. She felt her body respond at once, as though she had no control of it at all and she felt Bob pulling her down onto the soft grass. Dimly she felt the touch of the grass, cool, damp, against her legs and his warmth against her, hands caressing, setting her on fire. She wanted to pull away, to say no, that she wasn't ready for this, not yet, but another part of her refused. She had known desire often enough, known and answered its spell, but this was something more, a kind of flight that swept her along. Her lips were no longer merely answering but making demands of their own, and her body moved, twisted, writhed against his. A fervency about his touch, a burning haste, that with others would have made her rebel, only heightened the consuming urgency of the moment. Time was suddenly important to her, too, and for no reason at all, only that his hands were making it so, sweeping aside all else but their tactile message.

The whistling intruded like a shaft of lightning. She heard it first as though in a dream, and then it was frighteningly real, shocking, breaking the moment apart and she heard Bob's muttered *"Damn!"* as he pulled away. She half-rose to see the beam of a flashlight moving through the dark as the whistler approached. Straightening her dress, brushing back wisps of hair, feeling ridiculously like a high-school girl, she got to her feet with Bob as the whistling figure sauntered nearer.

"It's Glen, damn him," she heard Bob's savage whisper. "Damn his stupid hide."

Valery felt her deep breath released in a rush of air, and she stood very still, recoiling from her own thoughts. She'd not have stopped, she knew that. If Glen hadn't come by to interrupt she'd not have stopped. The thought didn't shock so much as it surprised and she looked up at Bob's intense handsomeness, tainted now with a hard anger that gave his face an edge of cruelty. She looked away to see the flashlight close now, making slow sweeps along the ground, rising to dance along the edge of a bush. Bob moved forward, out of the cluster of saplings, his hand holding hers and the flashlight swept over them, halted and moved back again to bathe them in its white light.

"Well, hello," Glen's voice called out as the beam of light dropped to the ground and he stepped closer. "This is a surprise. I didn't expect to meet anyone out here."

"Hello," Valery answered. "We were just strolling." Grimacing in the darkness, she wondered why she had felt it necessary to offer even a weak explanation.

"Brother Martin decided against chess," Glen said. "Found this light in the kitchen and thought I'd go for a walk. See you later maybe."

He waved the beam of light in a semi-circle, turned, and went on. The sound of his whistling drifted back to them as the light made a wide circle and then disappeared from view behind a line of trees. She glanced up at Bob.

"You could have said something. Hello, at least," she said.

"I didn't feel like saying anything," he answered, his voice hard. His hands on her shoulders, turning her to face him, but she moved back.

"I think it's time we went back," she said and saw the frown deepen on his face.

"I'm good at recapturing moods," he said.

"I'm sure of that. Too good," she replied. "I'm not giving you another chance. Not tonight, anyway."

She started away and Bob fell in beside her and she could feel the smoldering anger of him, as vibrant in its way as the other part of him had been.

"Damn him!" he muttered. "I'm going to send him on his way."

"Glen?" Valery protested. "That's not fair. He didn't do it on purpose."

"He's not necessary now."

"Not necessary?" Valery frowned. "What does that mean?" She caught Bob's moment of hesitation.

"For companionship, now that you're here," he answered.

"And so you just send him on his way after you invited him, just like that," Valery shot back, letting her angry disapproval stand open. Of course, Glen virtually asked for that kind of treatment, she added silently. She saw Bob's smile move across his face and reaching out, he pulled her to him.

"No, I guess not. I was just angry," he said, looking down at her as he held her against him. His kiss was quick, unexpected, and instantly stirring. "A reminder," he whispered. "And a down payment on next time."

She held herself against him. "I just like to be sure, that's all," she murmured.

"I'll make you sure," he said. "Waiting won't give you that answer."

"Maybe not," she admitted, stepping back. "We'll see."

The house was still when they reached it, and she saw the light out in Tansy's room. In the flickering lamplight of the hallway, with the gross, ornamental quality of the house even more oppressive than usual, she clung to Bob, again finding comfort in the singular sensuousness of his presence. Stepping back with an effort, she kissed him quickly and half ran up the steps to her room, closing the door behind her and leaning against it for a long minute. Undressing in the dark, she slid into the bed, still feeling the wanting in her body, remembering with her senses. He was different from anyone she'd ever known and in his arms, his hands on her, she had wanted nothing else. Yet, strangely, she'd been glad for Glen's interruption. Contradictory, yet completely true. But then everything here at *Verdelet* was contradictory, at odds with itself: ideas, architecture, and from what Fred had told her, events.

Slowly she felt her body relax and sleep began to pull upon her. Dark images tried to intrude, a twisted, grotesque object in the reeds, a little girl floating in a lake, silhouetted figures with hands raised in combat, but she pushed them all aside and finally lay still, jet hair against the whiteness of the pillow, as starkly contrasting as the colors of Tansy's room.

It was in the hushed hours of the night that she woke, almost two in the morning her watch on the bedside table told her. She felt dry, thirsty, her throat scratchy. Swinging from the bed, she went to the bathroom and downed a glass of water, a milk-white nymph in the darkness. Returning to the bed, she paused and went to the window to peer out. The moon had slipped behind the distant hills and the night was so much black ink. She was about to turn from the window when she saw the light, a pin-point first, flicking in the darkness, coming from the field this side of the small rise that led to the lake. The light moved nearer, became the thin finger of a flashlight beam. Who was wandering about at the hour? Not Glen still out there, Valery frowned, wishing the night were not so inky. The flashlight came closer and she watched, standing against the side of the window frame. Now the light was at the edge of the lawn and then, startling in its unexpectedness, it was turned off. Frowning in silent protest, Valery pressed forward, squinting in an effort to pierce the blackness. She thought she heard the sharp sound of a twig breaking under a footstep but she could see nothing. The wind blew in a sudden gust, rustling the leaves of the trees, and the night fell silent again. She waited but she could see nothing. Whoever it was had crossed the lawn by now. Moving to the door of her room she slipped the latch off noiselessly, opening the door a few inches to listen. She waited, holding her breath, listening for the sound of the front door being closed or footsteps in the halls below. But there was nothing, the house as silent as on all those nights when she'd waited there alone except for Labat. She closed the door, latching it again and returned to bed. It could well have been Labat, she thought. The man moved in silence. Tight-lipped, she turned her face into the pillow and closed her eyes. It could have been almost anyone, perhaps even a stranger walking past. She went to sleep wondering why whoever it was had turned off the light on reaching the lawn, plainly bent on staying unseen.

CHAPTER FIVE

Valery woke to find the morning cloudy, the view from her window laid over with grayness. But it was morning and morning always brought a brightness of the spirit, and she dressed in a jumpsuit of deep blue with yellow stitching. Hurrying downstairs, she found Glen in the kitchen over a mug of coffee he had brewed. His genial smile and soft eyes found her warming to him at once, brushing over the weakness she knew was part of him.

"Seen anyone yet this morning?" she asked. He shook his head and poured her a cup of coffee.

"No, not yet," he answered. "Sorry about last night."

"There's nothing to be sorry about," she said quickly. "You should have stayed and walked with us."

"Bob wouldn't have liked that," Glen smiled sheepishly.

"Oh, yes, I forgot, you don't do anything Bob doesn't like," Valery stabbed, ashamed of the crossness in her voice.

"I try not to," Glen said pleasantly. He was so completely content with his role it was infuriating. She abhorred weakness, especially in someone as attractive as Glen. She wondered, briefly, how he'd managed to come to her aid when the mare had run off with her.

"How are you getting on with Tansy?" he asked unexpectedly. Her answer came between sips of the steaming, waking coffee.

"She's a difficult child," Valery said. "I wonder how much this place has marked her. I wonder what affect the death of her parents has had on her. She was only four but some four-year-olds are very precocious. I have the feeling she was one of them. It was a family tragedy, I understand."

"Yes, her mother killed her father and then herself. There was talk that she'd also tried to kill the child before killing herself."

"How'd you learn all that?" Valery asked in surprise.

"I remembered the item in the newspapers when I first met Bob," Glen said smoothly, blandly.

"How perfectly awful for everyone involved," Valery said. "Was there any reason given for what happened? Had she a history of mental illness?"

"No, she was a nice, ordinary girl, as far as I can remember the accounts. Her sister testified that she had been increasingly upset about something but not even the sister knew what it was. The authorities finally put it down to a sudden emotional breakdown."

"But to try and kill her own child. That's ghastly."

"They said it was all done very quietly and calmly, as though she were doing a chore, something that needed to be done," Glen said.

Valery saw his eyes watching her and she shivered. "Awful, perfectly awful," she said. A tragedy indeed, she commented silently, entirely in keeping with the others, another part of the Van Dyne history of being pursued by tragedy. Were these things at least partially brought on by their affinity for death, she wondered. Or was it the other way around? How much did the excesses of the spirit of this ancestral mausoleum have to do with it all? Labat's entrance broke off her thoughts as his glance swept past Glen to rest on her and she felt the malevolence of the man again.

"Miss Tansy wants you. She is in her room," he said in his flat rasp. Valery rose and started from the room, Glen at her heels. Voices, raised and sharp, seeped from the closed door of the library as she reached the foot of the stairway, Bob's first, then Brother Martin.

"I guess I was wrong. Everyone is up and about," Glen said. "I just didn't see them."

Disconnected phrases sounded through the door. *"A little more time,* she heard Bob's voice say. *You know better … too many intangibles … find it someplace else.* Brother Martin's voice rose and fell. She started to turn to go up the stairs when the door opened and Bob called her. She turned to see his face tight, his thoughts still in his eyes as he let his smile shake them away.

"Best eye-opener I've seen this morning," he grinned. "Tansy has you for the day but I'm putting in my reservation for tonight."

Valery laughed, his breezy, vibrant charm impossible to ignore. "I'm going to spend the day grooming *Vodun,*" he said and then, turning to Glen, his smile flashed again. "What's on your agenda?" he asked.

"I'd just like to sit in the sun and relax," Glen said. "Even without the sun I'll settle for a nice camp chair on the terrace."

"Make it tomorrow. We need some things from town. You can go in with Labat and get them while he stays with the car," Bob said brusquely.

"Sure thing," Glen agreed. His soft eyes passed Valery for an instant and she turned away. *Puppet!* The word flashed silently across her mind. He didn't deserve his good looks, she commented to herself angrily, watching him follow Bob outside. She turned to start up the stairs again when she saw Tansy coming down, wearing her blue one-piece coverall. Her lips were edged with the same smile of secret wisdom she'd worn during dinner last night.

"Good morning," Valery sang out cheerfully. She received a condescending nod in return.

"I want to go down to the bogs this morning," Tansy announced.

"All right," Valery agreed, glad she'd decided to put on her thick-soled walking brogues. Her glance went down to the child's shoes and she saw the edging of darkness around them. "Your shoes are all wet already," she frowned.

"I was outside," Tansy said. "Early, in the dew. I woke up early and went outside."

"Then put on a pair of dry shoes. I'll wait here." Tansy shrugged and went back up the stairs. Valery watched the child in thought. Perhaps gentleness was not the best approach to Tansy. Perhaps boldness, putting her on the defensive, could reach through that disdainful air she held around herself like an invisible wall. She watched Tansy return, a pair of dry shoes on her feet, and she went outside with the child's spun-gold delicacy brightening the day as a jonquil brightens a patch of weeds. Tansy led the way to the bogs, moving surely across the hollow and through the tall grass of the high ridge that led to the swamp.

"What's so fascinating about the bogs, Tansy?" Valery asked as they walked. "They give me the shivers. The mist never leaves them and they're eerie."

"They're beautiful," Tansy corrected.

"No trying to go through them, remember," Valery said. "I'm assuming they'll be wrapped in mist as usual."

Tansy's small glance was disdainful and Valery returned it with the firm set of her jaw. As they crossed the high ridge and started down, the bogs lay before them, the bare arms of twisted trees reaching up from the mists like so many skeletons with hands upraised. This was its own small world, this dank, fog-shrouded spot. The marsh grass grew up from the water and acres of pitcher plants leaned outward, many of them easily within arm's reach.

"Look at that one," Tansy said delightedly, pointing to one of the cuplike plants with a dragonfly and a squashbug in its clutches, its leaves slowly closing around its victims. "I love pitcher plants," Tansy said. "Brother Martin says they are perfect organisms. They combine beauty and death, the beginning and the end."

"Did you ever think that perhaps Brother Martin's ideas are not all that wonderful?" Valery suggested. "All his talk about death and rejection and killing, that's nothing for a little girl your age."

Tansy's glance was condescending and Valery ignored it.

"I think you ought to spend more time with children your own age when you're here," Valery said. She hesitated a moment, watching Tansy reach out to pull a pitcher plant closer and peer inside it. "I know you had a friend from town," she said, deciding to plunge in. "I heard about that little girl."

The round, pale-blue orbs turned to look at her, unwavering, masked. "What did you hear?" Tansy asked, each word distinct, clipped off as with a shears.

"I just heard what happened to her," Valery said. "That's no reason why you shouldn't make new friends your own age here."

"I'm not interested."

"Didn't you like playing with that little girl?" Valery asked, keeping her voice casual. The round eyes were suddenly drops of blue ice.

"No."

The word was spat out coldly, the luminous eyes became the pinpoints of pure venom Valery had seen on the terrace.

"But she was your friend, I thought," Valery pressed, thoughts tearing themselves free in her mind, rushing out of the corners where she had pushed them with a will of their own, refusing to be held back.

"No, she wasn't," Tansy said coldly.

"Why do you say that? Because you'd argued that day?" Valery probed. "Just what did you argue about that day?"

Valery saw Tansy's eyes grow reflective, the pale blue becoming almost blue-white and distant.

"I told her I didn't want to climb anymore," Tansy said softly. A stillness wrapped itself around Valery. "I told her to come back to the house with me."

"And she refused," Valery supplied.

"She wanted to keep climbing trees," Tansy said. "I told her Carlotta would give us ice cream and cake."

"But she still refused," Valery said.

"I tried to pull her along with me and she kicked me. It hurt."

"You were trying to be nice to her and she turned on you," Valery said, her stomach tightly wound into a knot.

"I was trying to be nice to her," Tansy echoed.

"And she deserved what happened to her, didn't she?" Valery breathed. The luminous eyes blinked their assent.

"You reached out to her and she rejected you," Valery said.

"Yes," Tansy answered, a soft whispered word.

"Just like the cat," Valery breathed.

"Just like the cat.

"What happened then?" Valery asked, waiting the answer with a mixture of dread and hope. Tansy looked up at her fully and Valery saw the pale-blue eyes change expression, the sphinx-like mask slipping over them as she watched.

"I left," Tansy said quietly, staring at her. Valery let the two words roll back and forth across her mind. *I left.* Was that the truth? Or was that a hasty retreat? Had she really left then? Or had she stayed? And if she had stayed, what had actually happened then? The questions, now more chilling than before, hung in Valery's mind like so many vultures waiting to be satisfied. Certainly they hadn't been yet. The picture Tansy had revealed was sickeningly horrible, the implication of a terrible parallel. How far did it go? Rejection and killing, Brother Martin's thoughts again. To what loathsome lengths had they been carried? Perhaps it was best to leave the past alone, Valery thought. Certainly Tansy's story then had been true enough, with only a few parts left out and now those parts had been revealed to her. How vital were they, Valery asked herself again. How much did they say about what actually had happened that afternoon at the lake? Only one thing was clear. Tansy was either a child in desperate need of warmth and understanding or the epitome of evil.

Watching her caress one of the plants, a perfect picture of childlike loveliness, Valery wondered if she were indeed like one of the pitcher plants she liked so much, death wrapped in beauty, one of nature's deadly deceits.

Questions again, the same ones revolving inside her head like a lunatic carousel. Perhaps the answers to the important ones lay in the answers to the smaller ones. Perhaps they could at least furnish guideposts. If Tansy had indeed broken the cat's neck it would say something more about the child, and if she hadn't, Valery would be better able to help her. Certainly a veterinarian would be able to tell whether the cat had been slain by another animal. The tell-tale bites would have left marks somewhere to the trained eye. She would enlist Fred Wheaten's help. He could get the cat's body and take it to a local veterinarian. But only after she'd spoken to him of Tansy's dinner-table remarks about secret meetings. That would come first. She glanced at her watch and saw that the morning had passed quickly. She was just about to call the child when Tansy strolled over to her.

"I want to go back," Tansy said. "I'm very tired. I want to take a nap."

"Of course," Valery said. "Let's go at once." She let Tansy lead the way and the child was silent. Valery wondered if the questions about the tragedy of the little girl had upset her. They were almost back at the house when Tansy finally spoke again.

"I'm going to sleep," the child said. "I'll stay in my room the rest of the day."

Valery glanced sharply at the child but Tansy's perfect-featured little face revealed nothing. It was most unusual for a child to suddenly feel so tired, any child, unless they were actually ill and Tansy showed no signs of that. There wasn't the slightest hint of a flush of fever on her alabaster skin. Her eyes didn't even show tiredness. Why the sudden attack of exhaustion, Valery wondered. Flight? A hasty retreat from further questions? The awareness of having said more than she'd intended and the need for time and quiet to prepare her story again? All possibilities and yet they didn't feel right. Valery knew she should be pleased at Tansy's desire to sleep. It was a stroke of luck, her chance to slip away to meet Fred Wheaten without trying to find some excuse to get away. And yet she felt uneasy. They went into the house and Labat passed them with some rags. She saw Glen out of the corner of her eye, leaning against the fender of the vintage Ford half-out of the stable.

"I think I'll stay in my room the rest of the day," Tansy said as they went upstairs. "I'll probably sleep most of the time."

"Good," Valery said, pushing open the door. "I'll look in on you before dinner and we can decide then if you ought to come down or not."

She watched the child undress, a supple steel-wire strength to her slender figure, Valery noted. Tansy seemed suddenly very much the little girl and Valery closed the door as she left, noting the door latched only from inside, as the one in her room. "I'll tell the others not to disturb you," she said and a last glance backward showed Tansy atop her bed already. Valery went down the stairs with her lips tight. The child was a paradox, cold and contemptuous, hinting at monstrous evil, and a lost little girl of exquisite beauty. Learning about the cat was consumingly important, the key to everything else. Determination and shamefulness were a mixed-up ball inside herself, strange bedfellows indeed. What had seemed so sickeningly clear at the bogs was no less so now and yet here, seeing Tansy in her room, the small slenderness of her, it all seemed just impossible to accept. Hurrying to her room, she flung herself across the bed and closed her eyes. She had hours before it was time to slip away to meet Fred Wheaten. She would try not to think, to lie in that middle-land between wakefulness and slumber, letting time nudge the day along.

It refused to cooperate, her mind, time, the loud silence of the house, none of them cooperating. Finally she rose to pace the room, then to press cold water against her face in the bathroom. One thought above all others pressed on her. Tansy's sudden desire for sleep, for being alone. Was the child being particularly clever? Had it been a pretext so she could slip out and take up a spot to spy on her? If so, it would mean that Tansy's dinner-table remarks were more than the empty comments of a precocious child. It would mean that she strongly suspected or knew of the secret meetings between herself and Fred Wheaten. And, of course, Valery grimaced, she'd have to put off her plans to slip away to meet Fred. The girl glanced at her watch. If that indeed had been Tansy's scheme, the child would have to have slipped out of the house by now. Valery went to the door and listened for sounds below. The house was quite still. Labat and Glen would have left for the village by now, and Bob was in the stables. That left only Brother Martin. Valery crept down the stairs, paused at the bottom and then darted to the opposite stairway, taking the steps two-at-a-time on the balls of her feet. At the top of the landing she moved forward slowly, halting at Tansy's room. The doorknob in Valery's hand was cold, making her skin flinch for a second and she turned it slowly, carefully, until she heard the small sound of the latch. She pressed in on the door. It didn't move. Keeping a firm grip on the turned doorknob, she pressed harder. The door held. It was latched from inside.

Valery felt the relieved rush of her breath. Tansy was inside the room. Valery let the knob slowly turn back and then she hurried from the door. She went down the steps and across the foyer, her hand reaching for the front door when the gray-robed figure stepped from the library.

"Valery, my dear," he said. "I've been wanting to have a talk with you about something. I hear Tansy's not feeling well?"

"A little overtired, perhaps," Valery said.

Brother Martin's hand was on her arm, guiding her into the library. She saw a teapot and cups on the small table as he guided her to the sofa. "Robert tells me I upset you last night," Brother Martin said. "You must forgive me, my dear, especially after your earlier upset in the afternoon. I'm so often carried away by my own convictions. I do tend to sermonize, an occupational carryover, I'm afraid."

Valery kept the panic from showing on her face as she cast about for some excuse to refuse. Nothing even remotely believable came to mind.

"And we have seen so much of that worse side of human nature here at *Verdelet*," he went on, pouring a cup of tea for her. "Naturally, I have strong feelings about the absolute truth of my words. But here I go again, carrying on. I really called you in to get some answers from you about Tansy."

Valery kept her face calm as she churned inside. Fred Wheaten would be arriving at the little glen behind the birches. She put the teacup Brother Martin handed her at the edge of the table, echoing the way she sat poised for flight.

"Tansy is a most unusual child. We all recognize that," he said. "I'm wondering what opinions you may have formed about her so far."

"None I'm ready to talk about yet," Valery said quickly and then, seeing Brother Martin's quizzical glance, softened her abruptness quickly. "That is, no opinions that are defined enough to put into words. I need more time to study the child."

She took a sip of the tea and glanced at her watch as she raised the cup, her mind racing to find an excuse that would get her out of the house. She was drawing a blank, she realized. There just wasn't anything plausible, any logical reason that would make it necessary for her to rush off.

"Carlotta is not well, you know," Brother Martin droned on. He eased his big bulk into one of the chairs with a finality that made the girl wince inwardly. "If it were necessary, could you stay on longer with Tansy?" he asked. "Plans for her schooling this year are still indefinite."

"I don't know. I'd have to think about it," Valery said, listening to the minutes tick away.

"I think it would be good for Tansy. I think it would be good for you. I believe you might even have a sense of mission and that's what is needed for so many things in this world. There are so few today who have a sense of mission. Modern society seems to have reduced that aspect of human character, along with a good many others."

"Your years with the Church have given you that?" Valery commented.

"Only partly so, my dear, only partly so," Brother Martin said. "My sense of mission has many roots, shall we say?" He smiled, settled himself again, and went off onto another topic, the relationship of children to adults in modern society. Valery interspersed polite comments at the proper time while her heart continued to plummet. It was nearly four-thirty, her watch told her, and she was still hopelessly trapped. Finally, as Brother Martin shifted topics again, she stood up.

"I think Bob is waiting for me," she said. "I really ought to go and find out."

"Bob's in the stables and he hates being disturbed when he's grooming the horses." The smile was a patient, friendly warning.

"Well, I think I'll go out and see if he's outside. Maybe he's finished." It was crude, obvious, and she fumed silently at her own ineptitude.

Brother Martin's smile grew expansive. "Well, perhaps you ought to go on anyway, get a little time for yourself before Tansy wakes. We can talk more about this tomorrow."

"Yes, yes, of course," she said, the words rushing from her and then she was in the hall, yanking the front door open, rushing out into the grayness of the afternoon. Forcing herself not to run, she skirted the stables. She couldn't risk meeting Bob and another delay. It would be nearly five before she reached the meeting place, her hopes now concentrated on praying that he'd waited. Once past the stables she cut across the field and onto the road out of the hollow, half-walking, half-running. Topping the rise that marked the end of the hollow, the road lay ahead in a series of gentle curves, the trees bordering both sides of it. Raising little whorls of dust as she hurried on, she turned the last of the curves before the silver birches to see a small knot of figures directly in front of her. They were abreast of the birches and she saw the three men nearest turn to watch her approach. Beyond them she saw the police car with its red signal light on the roof blinking like a huge, bloodshot eye. Lowering her glance, she saw the blanket-covered figure sprawled across the road, the sight of it sent a shiver through her automatically, the feel of death about the shrouded form. One of the men, tall, a hawklike face, moved toward her. He wore a light gray fedora and a light topcoat. Her eyes mirrored her questions and surprise. "Good day, miss," the man said softly. "I'm Sheriff Huxley of Lakeview. There's been some trouble, I'm afraid."

Valery grimaced inwardly. This settled it. Either Fred had left or, if he was inside the little glen behind the birches she'd no way to get to him now. "Trouble?" she asked. She saw a second police cruiser coming up the road behind the tall, thin man.

"I'm afraid so," he nodded. "May I have your name?"

"Valery Curtis," the girl answered. "I'm at the Van Dynes', taking care of the child." She kept her gaze on the sheriff, not daring to look toward the glen, wondering if Fred was waiting in there.

"A man's been killed," the sheriff said quietly and Valery felt her eyes widen. "Murdered, to be accurate," he added. With one quick motion he bent down and pulled the blanket from the form under it. "Do you know this man?" he asked.

Valery stared down at the lifeless form, at the affable face twisted in pain, at the ruler sticking from the hip pocket. She let her eyes stare for a long moment at the hilt of the knife protruding from the base of the man's neck, plunged in from the back and she heard her voice as though it came from a distant place.

"My God! Oh, my God," she whispered. "It's Fred Wheaten," *It's Fred Wheaten.* The words repeated silently inside her and the world was spinning. She felt the tall man's hand catch her as she swayed, steadying her. Her knees had turned to water and she was glad for his hand holding her.

"You knew Wheaten?" she heard Sheriff Huxley say and she gathered strength from someplace and stopped swaying.

"Just casually. I've stopped in at the Wheatens' cottage. It's down the road toward town."

"We know. We've sent a man down to notify his wife," the man said. His thin face looked down at her, his eyes appraising. Valery kept her eyes averted from the form across the road, still unable to grasp more than the bare outlines of what she had seen, the world still spinning, the whole thing unreal.

"We've determined he was stabbed in a small glen just the other side of these birches," the sheriff said. "Apparently left for dead, he managed to crawl out here to the road. A farmboy passing found him and called us. It was too late by then, of course. It looks as though he was meeting someone in the glen where he was stabbed."

Secret lovers. Secret meetings. Tansy's words reverberated in her head. Was Fred really meeting someone else here at the glen. He had chosen the spot for their meetings, their French lessons. Did he use it for other purposes, too? Her mind automatically rejected the thought. He wasn't that kind of man. It made no sense, none of it.

"Where were you going just now, Miss Curtis?" The sheriff's voice was casual, the question less so.

"Nowhere. I was just out for a walk," Valery lied. The instinct for self-preservation was instant and automatic, she realized in some surprise. To say she'd been on her way to meet Fred

Wheaten would plunge her into a morass of involvement and implications, she told herself. It would turn something entirely innocent and well-meaning into a focus of skepticism. It would do no good for anyone or anything. She might even be disbelieved entirely. It would be just her story, totally unsupported, unusual enough under ordinary circumstances. She might, and she felt her throat go dry, be suspected, perhaps even accused. She felt the sheriff's hand tighten on her arm.

"Sorry you came along just now," he said. "Bit rough, this kind of thing. Shall I have one of my men take you back?"

"No, no thank you. I'll be all right," she said quickly. "Walking back will help."

"Whatever you say, Miss Curtis," the man said, his eyes penetrating, intent. "If you can think of anything that might be helpful please call my office in Lakeview. We'll be stopping at the Van Dynes' for routine questioning. We'll be doing that with everyone in the area, I'm afraid."

"Of course," she said, turning, walking away slowly, fighting down the impulse to run. Fred Wheaten's lifeless face swam in front of her and she walked as though in a dream, the horror of what had happened seeping through to her in ever-increasing waves of nausea. Fred Wheaten murdered. The impact so stunned it made thinking a jumbled, disorganized process. Had it been done by someone he'd gone there to meet? Or had it happened while he was waiting to meet her? Perhaps he'd been waiting patiently for her and was attacked from behind by a thief, a passing lunatic who had stumbled upon him. *Secret lovers, secret meetings.* Tansy's words came back again. Did the child really know anything? The answer was more important than ever now.

Reaching the house, she saw that the vintage Ford was still gone and she hurried past the stables. She was almost at the front door when it opened and Bob stood there, his eyes darkening at once as he saw the strain on her face.

"What is it?" he asked quickly, his arms holding her, comforting, reassuring.

"Someone was killed, *murdered*," she said into his chest. "Fred Wheaten, the carpenter who lived down the road. I came on the police at the scene when I was walking."

"You poor kid," Bob murmured, and she lifted her head to see his face drawn, a tight line around his lips and almost a resignation in his eyes.

"Another tragedy on your doorstep," she half whispered, a rush of sympathy flooding over her. Bob nodded slowly.

"It seems that way, doesn't it?" he said. "Did you know the man?"

That question again. Her answer came smoothly now, taking on its own kind of truth. "Only casually," she said. "The sheriff said he'd have someone stop by for routine questioning."

"Of course," Bob answered. She held herself close against him.

"I think I'm going to lie down awhile," she said. "I'll look in on Tansy, first."

"I just did. She's still asleep. You go on up to your room and lie down. I'll see you at dinner," Bob answered and she stepped back, turned away, and went up the stairs, wanting to go back to his arms and tell him everything. But she dared not, certainly not until she knew more. Tansy was his flesh and blood. Valery knew how she herself had been sickened by the ultimate conclusions about the child, still unwilling to accept the possibility her mind had drawn in frightful logic. Certainly Bob would be more unwilling to accept it on unproven suspicions. And now there was Fred Wheaten's murder and Tansy's cryptic remarks. Silence was still her refuge, Valery decided. Logic, not fear, dictated her course. Entering the room, she felt the perspiration coating her skin and she took off the outfit to lie on the bed in bra and panties, feeling the air shrivel up the little beads of water on her body. Death! The ugly word seemed indigenous to this place, this hollow of land, and now it had reached out to touch her. But she wouldn't panic. She would wait, be careful. To know what Tansy's comments meant was the first step. If there was another woman, another secret meeting, and the child knew about it, then there'd be no need to tell about the innocent times when she and Fred had met behind the birches. There'd be only the conversation at the bogs and the chilling, sickening implications of it. That was burden enough to wrestle with, Valery told herself.

A sound outside broke off her thoughts and she went to the window to see Labat and Glen arriving in the old Ford. Glen, packages in his arms, spoke excitedly to Brother Martin and Bob as they emerged from the house. Valery saw Tansy appear, wearing a black velvet jumper, looking fresh and delicately lovely. Glen was speaking excitedly and she knew of what. They would have had to pass the grisly scene on the road back from town. She saw the small knot of figures break up, Glen the last to disappear from her line of vision, his face clouded, serious. Valery turned from the window. It was not a subject that would be ignored during dinner and perhaps that was all for the best, distasteful as it would be to her. It might elicit enough from Tansy to clarify her cryptic remarks. She could hope, anyway. She lay down again, waiting, not wanting to go down too soon. Finally, putting on a simple dress, deep green with a zippered front, she went downstairs to find the others in the library. Bob had made drinks and handed her one as she entered. Tansy, she noted, sat in a high-backed chair with a dish of crackers in her lap, looking beautiful, doll-like.

"Feeling better?" Bob asked. She nodded.

"I understand you were first to bring the exciting news, my dear," Brother Martin said. "You seem to have a talent for coming upon upsetting sights."

Valery met Glen's eyes and saw they were intent on her. "It was all over town before we left," he said.

"The whole thing's like a bad dream. I still can't believe it," Valery said. "Who would do such a thing? It must have been a maniac, someone he came upon unexpectedly."

"It was a lovers' quarrel."

Tansy's voice, soft steel cutting through the room.

"Tansy! What a thing to say?" Valery threw back.

"It's true," Tansy said evenly. "A woman killed him." The spun-gold figurine toyed with a cracker, her comments delivered with idle nonchalance. Valery kept her voice from rising.

"Where do you get all this information?" she asked.

"The police found an earring in his hand," Tansy tossed off airily. "Labat heard about that in town. They must have struggled before she killed him."

Valery forced a smile as a knot in her stomach formed. "Tansy, you mustn't believe wild rumors and gossip," she said. "People say all sorts of things about things like this."

"It's not gossip. They found the earring in his hand," Tansy defended.

"Secret meetings again?" Valery chided while the knot grew larger and tighter.

"They met every day in that little meeting place off the road."

Valery wondered if the others could hear the pounding of her pulse, and she kept the small smile fixed on her lips. What meetings, the voice inside her screamed in silence. Did Tansy mean her meetings with Fred or was she talking of someone else? Was there a someone else?

"How do you know all these things, Tansy?" Valery plunged.

"I just know."

The answer, suddenly childish, almost petulant, evasive, infuriated. Was it an admission that she really knew nothing at all? Vallery was glad for Brother Martin's interruption.

"Next thing you'll be telling us you know who the woman is?" he chuckled.

"Maybe I do," Tansy said, the childish petulance still in her voice. Brother Martin's tone became chiding.

"Now, now, Tansy, careful of that kind of talk. Why, if there is a woman involved and she killed the man, that sort of talk could make you a target," he admonished.

Valery saw the child's enigmatic smile and saw the pale-blue saucers brush past her in a brief glance. She felt a shock as she realized that a surge of pure hatred was coursing through her for this angel-faced child. Hatred was the spawn of fear, she realized, and she feared Tansy now, for reasons she could define and for others less clear. She had glimpsed behind the child's facade and had turned away in horror at what she saw, unwilling to believe in what appeared to be real. But had she turned away? Had she made her own conclusions without admitting them to herself? Labat entered the room to announce that dinner was ready and Valery turned off her thoughts. Bob was at her side, his words idle chatter which she answered with smiles and comments dredged up from habit. Even his commanding personality failed to sweep away the chill that had taken hold of her and all she could think of were Tansy's remarks, more cryptic than the others, more pointed then before. But no more revealing.

Dinner was a kind of hell with talk and speculation about the killing, about Fred Wheaten, about murder itself. She caught Glen's eyes on her a number of times and she was glad for the softness in them, an understanding that showed he saw her dislike of the topic. Brother Martin found a relish in the subject she should have expected but which nonetheless irritated.

"You sound almost as if you admire those who kill," she heard herself snap at one point, instantly sorry she sounded so on edge.

"Murderers? Killers? I must admit a fondness for them. Philosophically, of course." He beamed. "They are imbued with the eschatological viewpoint, too. They have embraced the philosophy of the importance of the last things, those finalities again.

But subconcsiously, of course, my dear, always subconsciously. You see, killing may be an emotional act but it's a philosophical statement, the embrace of a viewpoint. The act itself is triggered emotionally but that's because we always reject intellectual decisions when they involve us personally. We are bothered by their lack of humanity so we make them and let them stand, like a pie cooling on a rack, until our emotions come to supply the excuse we need."

Valery sniffed disdainfully. "And that always happens," she half sneered. Brother Martin's smile was benign.

"Invariably," he said. "All those dark shepherds see to that. Once we have given ourselves to them, even a little bit, we are theirs."

Valery caught Tansy's luminous eyes on her and felt almost sympathy for the child. How much had this spurious friar's wild philosophizing added to Tansy's inner problems, she wondered. She closed her ears to further talk and dinner was over and she'd lived through it with outward composure masking her inner turmoil.

"I want to see you alone," she heard Bob's whisper as they headed for the doorway. "I'll make you forget all this."

"Maybe later," she said, not entirely without honesty. It would be good to let his strength shut out the unreality of this private world. "Right now I want to see that Tansy gets up to her room and stays there. This thing has her imagination all wound up. Then I'm going to rest a while myself."

"You do that right now," Bob said. "I'll see that Tansy gets to her room and undressed."

Valery paused and then nodded agreement, welcoming any chance to get away and think alone. Besides, she had no wish to confront Tansy alone yet, not until she had set a course of action. She watched Bob catch up to where the child and Brother Martin were already crossing the hallway and she turned to find Glen beside her.

"You seem all tensed up, not that I blame you," he said, his eyes wide, guileless. "Don't let it get to you."

His genial affability was hardly what she needed now. "I'll try not to," she said curtly and left him, hurrying up to her room. *Don't let it get to you,* he had said. It was inside her, consuming her, tearing her apart. Standing at the window, she stared into the night as she assembled her thoughts. Tansy still held the first answers on which everything else depended. Perhaps the answers could be pried from her. Boldness had made the child open up earlier at the bogs, more than she had wanted to, Valery reflected. Maybe it would do the same now. She waited a few moments more, making certain she left time for Bob to leave the child, and then she went into the hallway and down the steps. The library, off to the side, didn't open directly onto the front hallway and she crossed the area to the east stairs, hastening up them to Tansy's room. Taking a deep breath, she knocked and entered without waiting an answer, closing the door after her. The child was sitting cross-legged on the black satin quilt. The child watched Valery approach, something close to mocking amusement swimming in the depths of the pale-blue eyes. Once again she was surprised at the surge of anger she felt as she met Tansy's stare.

"I think a little talk is in order," Valery said crisply. "You know, Tansy, little girls often have an overactive imagination that makes unreal things seem real. It often carries them away with themselves and makes them say more than they actually know."

Tansy's eyes held their cool amusement. "Like secret meetings and secret lovers?" she queried.

"Yes, and about earrings in peoples' hands."

"Oh, but there was an earring. Labat even heard a description of it. Wood with gold trim, sort of a half-moon shape. You had a pair like that, didn't you?"

Valery felt ice coating her anger and a gnawing fear inside her. "I lost one of my earrings at the lake and you know it," Valery said. "If there was an earring in Fred Wheaten's hand it wasn't mine. The one in my jewelry box will prove that and if they like they can comb the reeds by the lake and find the other one." Valery felt a sudden flood of relief rush over her. There *were* answers, she had discovered.

"Only it's not down there," Tansy said calmly.

"What are you talking about?" Valery asked.

"Your earring. It's not down by the reeds." The child's utter calm was enraging.

"Of course it's down there," Valery bristled.

"It was in Fred Wheaten's hand. The police have it now," Tansy said, the opaque blue circles dancing with little flames in the centers. Valery suddenly felt the ice drench her body and in her mind she saw a flashlight beam in the night. It had approached the house from the rise that led to the lake.

"It was you," she gasped. "That's why your shoes were all wet this morning, from tramping about in the night dew." Valery felt numbing shock drop over her like a net. Tansy's words were unbelievable lies that, even as she heard them, were beyond her power to repair or refute.

"You and Fred Wheaten were secret lovers," Tansy said calmy.

"No!" Valery tore the word out.

"You met every day at that meeting place you had behind the birches," Tansy went on smoothly.

"No, no, not as lovers," Valery cried in denial. "It wasn't that way at all."

"You were lovers and you quarreled and you killed him."

"No!" Valery heard the child's words through a spinning, numbed world. "You can't say a thing like that. It's not true."

"It is if I say it is," Tansy replied. "You were seen meeting him every day. Your earring was in his hand. Who do you think will believe you?"

Tansy was smiling now, a cold, perfect, contained smile of disdain. Valery felt her fury explode, the surge of hate she had built up inside for this strange child erupting out of control. Her hand shot out and she heard the sharp sound of it slapping Tansy across the face.

"What are you trying to do, you vicious little child?" she screamed and then she struck out again. Tansy fell back on the bed and her hands shot out to grab Valery's wrists. The girl felt her wrists being twisted by fingers like steel rods, fingers with inordinate strength, powerful enough to break the neck of a cat. Or a little girl? The question flew by as she tore her wrists free of Tansy's grip and stood before the child, her arm still upraised to strike again, trembling in something more than fury. In the cold, Siamese cat's eyes she saw cold triumph and, bringing her arm down she turned and ran from the room slamming the door after her. The strange triumph in Tansy's eyes ran along with her as she flew down the steps, stopping at the bottom as she heard the voices coming from the library. She drew a deep breath, crossed the hallway in a half-run and moments later yanked open the door of her room, flinging herself on the bed. Lying there face down, she felt the bed shake with the trembling of her body. Slowly, the shaking came to a stop and she raised herself to sit up on the bed. She had gotten answers, terrible answers that defied explanation.

Valery let her mind straighten itself out enough to try and think logically. Somehow Tansy knew of her meetings with Fred Wheaten. Unexplainable, impossible as it was, she knew. There was no longer any room to doubt that. The earring lost in the reeds by the lake had found its way into Fred Wheaten's lifeless hand. Had Tansy put it there herself? After plunging the knife into the base of the man's neck? She would have held a handkerchief around the hilt of the knife, of course. The child was terribly clever. But she was still a child, neither strong enough nor tall enough to plunge the knife so deeply into a man's neck. And she had been locked inside her room, the door latched from the inside. She'd seen that for herself. Labat could have done it for her but he had been in town with Glen. It had to have been Tansy. She'd as much as admitted having retrieved the earring. Unless there was yet someone else, someone she didn't know existed. Valery felt her hands clench into fists, her lips draw tight on her face.

She rose and went to the window, her eyes probing the darkness. She had to know about Tansy first. There had to be another way out of the child's room but she had to be certain. The child would be asleep later. She had to take the chance. It would at least confirm one thing in this place of questions without answers, of implications that curdled the mind. It would prove that Tansy was there, at least, alone or with someone else. The loathsome conclusions she had pushed aside at the bogs could no longer be pushed away. There was an evil here, and it had a name. The child had all but revealed the truth of what had happened that afternoon at the bogs to the little girl from town. Her last moment withdrawal into the safety of her original story had been too late and the child knew it. Valery felt her wrists still throbbing from where Tansy's fingers had clutched them. Tansy was physically capable of hurting, all right. The twisted neck of the cat and the twisted neck of the little girl, payments for rejection.

By now, it was beyond believing, and yet beyond denying, the actions rising from a diseased psyche. The child was a twisted, warped killer and now she had cleverly and coldly framed Valery as a murderess. She wondered about the child's reasons, if pure evil needed a reason for its actions. Certainly she'd never rejected the child's friendship. There never had been any, really, she reflected, not from the very first day of her arrival. There had only been the cold, disdainful hauteur. And now this, a clever move that had been planned with deliberate care, making her appear a murderess. It made no sense, no more than the strange look of triumph in Tansy's eyes when she had slapped her. That didn't fit anyplace, either. Why should Tansy want Valery to be thought a murderess? Why kill an innocent man to construct her macabre plot? The question asked itself again and as it did, an answer shot across the girl's mind and she turned from the window. Of course, Valery gasped silently. That had to be it. The admission she had made at the bogs, the truths she had carefully covered over and suddenly let slip. This was her countermove, checkmate by murder, monstrously in keeping with her sick mind.

Valery bit her lower lip. Of course, this precarious balance, this *quid pro quo* via death, could not be let stand, not for long. Tansy could not let it stay there. Unless, Valery pondered, the child hoped for a Satan's bargain, a trading off of murders, one lie for the other. And the child held all the weapons with which to bargain. What if she went to the sheriff? Would he believe her? Would he believe her story of why she and Fred Wheaten had met secretly? She saw his thin, skeptical face as he had watched her approach along the road, the probing eyes trained not for acceptance, not for trust, but for disbelief and suspicion. *Where were you going just now, Miss Curtis?* he had asked. If he knew the earring in the slain man's hand was hers would he believe she'd just been out walking? Or would he conclude she had discovered the loss of it and was hurrying back to retrieve it? She grimaced, knowing the answer. She would as much as confess if she came forward now, holding only a thin story against the earring and Tansy's exposure of their secret meetings. The thought of the child set her anger surfacing at once. She had to risk entering the child's room tonight. There had to be a hidden exit, a wall stairwell, some way that would prove it had been possible for the child to slip out of the house and go to the glen to set up her deadly trap.

Tansy was the key to virtually everything, and there she had only inner certainty, not proof. Her only hope lay in finding a way to Tansy, in convincing the child she couldn't win, or go on forever in her sickness. She shuddered at the prospect. The child was ice. How did one reach the heart of an iceberg? Was it a hopeless attempt, doomed before even trying?

Yet Valery had nothing else left to try. The unreality of it all gathered her own cold anger inside her. To come here had been a chance happening, an impulsive act and then the house with its unnerving, overwrought oppressiveness, the month alone and then the strangeness of the child. It had been a chain of its own and she had forged the first link. *Are you so preoccupied with paying back?* She heard her father's question again, and now there was no place left for denials. She had wanted to hurt, but not like this. She'd only wanted to hurt on her terms, when she could live with the distastefulness of it, enjoying her small triumphs of rejection with only enough guilt feelings to keep balance. But that had gotten out of hand even before she'd taken the old dowager's offer, she knew. And now, everything was out of hand. She could even see the headlines. Prominent Architect's Daughter Murderess! She would have killed her father by that, she knew. Even if, by some chance, she were cleared, the deed would have been done. Acquittals were so often such pyrrhic victories. His reputation would be shattered beyond repair, a lifetime of work capped by a scandal that would cling forever. Valery felt the anger seething. She wouldn't let it happen. Not just for herself. That suddenly seemed less important. She'd reach the little monster in one way or another. Tansy would kill nothing else in this world.

The knock on the door broke off her thoughts and she answered to see Bob, in shirt-sleeves, his intense handsomeness overwhelming in its vibrance. His eyes burned with a deep glow and his hand reached for her at once, pulling her toward him and she felt the animal strength and warmth of the man. "I got tired of waiting," he said. "I've brandies in the library. I thought you'd like one. The others have all turned in."

She let Bob pull her from the room, his arm around her waist exciting, his firm pressure dictating a message of its own. In the library she sank onto the leather couch and let the brandy flow through her. She saw Bob turn the latch on the door and then he was beside her, his physical vibrancy electric. "I think it's time we stopped waiting," he said softly. "Too much thinking is no good, I told you that." She nodded. He was like a breath of air, not pure, clean air, but the wildness of a storm that attracted, that made you want to embrace its power. "Forget about everything but us," he whispered. "Shut out the world. Make believe it doesn't exist."

It was a more than appealing thought. "How do you do that?" she murmured.

"Like this," he whispered and she felt his lips on hers, opening her mouth, holding her lips parted while he made soft demands of his own. It was more than just his sensuousness, more than just the instant desires he could arouse with his touch. It was herself, a reckless flight that was in her. His lips, his arms, his hands on her were a call to forget everything else, if only for a moment, a kind of refuge of the senses. She'd felt it before in his arms, and now it swept over her and, despite an inner disapproval, she matched his wildness. Perhaps he, like some rare men, was tuned to a woman's emotions and knew when all they had to do was to be there at the right time. Or perhaps he alone made her come alive like flame, wanting to consume and to be consumed in the process. She didn't care, but answered his every demand, her own hands caressing as fervently as his.

His lips were tracing little paths of ecstacy down along the smooth skin of her shoulder and she knew the dress had come open when the doorknob turned, a rasping, intruding sound. She felt Bob pull away, his head come up, and she turned to see the knob of the door turning again. Then the door moved as someone outside pressed against it, trying to open it. The knob was rattled now, the door leaned on again and she pulled the dress closed automatically.

"Damn! Now who locked the door?" she heard the muffled voice from the other side. "You can't even get a book to read."

It was Glen's voice and then, after a final turn of the knob, she heard his footsteps move away. It was the second time he had interrupted and again she was strangely glad for it. Bob relaxed and he turned to reach for her again. She slipped away to stand up and she saw his frown. "Don't be ridiculous," Bob said. "Sit down, Valery."

"I'm not being ridiculous," Valery answered. She saw his dark eyes searching hers, frowning, and she knew that she had no answers she could give him now, only that it would be wrong.

"I'm sorry, Bob," Valery tried. "It's not the time. It was best we were interrupted. It would have been wrong, all wrong, believe me."

"It would have been wonderful," he said and there was a muted savagery to his voice.

"Yes, wonderful but all wrong," she admitted. "I can't explain more now but you'll understand—I know you will. Maybe there'll be a right time."

He rose and she watched his face harden with that tight smile edging his lips. "It was a bad idea from the start," he said bitterly.

She frowned. "Why do you say that?" she protested.

"Because it was. Some ideas are just bad, like mixing business with pleasure. It never really works out."

"I guess now it's my turn not to understand," she frowned.

"That makes us even, doesn't it?" he said, going to the door and unlocking it. "See you tomorrow, Valery," he said, leaving abruptly. The girl hesitated, her lips pressed together tightly, wanting to run after him and bring him back. After a few minutes, she walked slowly from the room, wondering about the bitter meaning of his words.

She had almost reached the top of the stairs when the gaunt figure appeared and she stopped, startled. Labat, a broom in his hand, moved past her noiselessly in the semidarkness at the top of the steps but she saw his eyes go over her in a split-second appraisal. He was hardly sweeping in the darkness at this hour, she mused. Perhaps he was retrieving the broom from wherever he'd left it earlier. She watched him go down the stairs and out the front door, silent and malevolent, and she hurried into her room, latching the door quickly.

Feeling drained, exhausted, she undressed quickly, her body still filled with the echoes of desire. Going to the dresser for her hairbrush her glance swept over the little jewelry box. It was open, the lid upraised, the small rows of pins and jewelry visible. She gasped in surprise. The other earring was gone. She'd carefully put it away, hoping the lost one might be found, and now it was gone, too. Labat, she said silently. That's what he'd been doing, stealing the other earring for Tansy. The gaunt servant and the child had their own evil partnership. Was that how Tansy knew she'd been meeting with Fred in the glen every day for almost a month? Had Labat been the one to tell her? Valery thought back of how she always checked behind her and looked up and down the road before stepping into the birches. Besides, most of the time Labat had been at the house when she'd gone walking to the glen. Silent as he was, she'd have been aware of his following her in broad daylight, she felt certain. Or would she have? She furrowed her brow at her own uncertainty about things she thought were certain.

Valery sat down in a chair and waited, letting the hours grow deeper. Labat had stolen the earring for Tansy, which meant the child had a plan for it. Maybe she could foil that much at least. The gaunt hulk of a man had taken the earring back to his room over the stables until morning when he could pass it to Tansy. Maybe she could prevent that. But first, now, she had to know how Tansy could have left her room with the door latched.

Finally, when the night was at its deepest, she rose and crept downstairs and up the east stairway to the child's room. Trying the door, hoping the child hadn't latched it again, she felt it give and she stepped into the dark room. Moonlight filtered through the window and outlined shapes clearly. She saw Tansy asleep in the big bed and she stepped toward it. Valery stared down at the child and felt her body trembling, her mind a whirling, racing jumble of thoughts she refused to heed. She turned away quickly, pulling herself from the bed and crossing the room. She pressed her hands along first one wall, then another. Pausing every few moments to glance at the child, Valery circled the room as Tansy slept soundly, hardly stirring. The walls were solid, holding no secret stairway. The girl went into the first of two closets in the room pushing her way through the child's dresses hanging there. The closet revealed nothing and the second one was equally unproductive. Valery moved carefully across the floor, step-by-step, pressing down with each step, trying to feel a floor board that moved, that gave way a little. Small dots of perspiration grew on her forehead and she wiped them away with the back of her hand as she finished criss-crossing the floor. Tansy suddenly stirred, turned over, and Valery froze against the wall, half-hidden behind the dresser. But the child didn't wake and the girl moved from the wall again.

There was nothing here—no hidden stairway, no secret passage that led from the room. But there had to be a way out of the room while the door stayed latched. Tansy was the only one who could have committed the slaying. It was her trap, she had set up all the parts, and everyone else was accounted for this afternoon, Bob, Labat and Glen, and she had been with Brother Martin herself. Unless, and Valery felt her breath catch, Tansy had someone else, someone she'd never met nor heard of as a secret accomplice. Valery shook away the thought angrily. She was clutching at straws, she told herself. Somehow, Tansy had gotten out of this room with the door latched. The child had set up the situation, feigning tiredness, wanting to spend the afternoon undisturbed and sleeping. Valery started for the door as Tansy turned again. She had stretched her luck now. It was time to leave. She was at the door when a sudden movement caught her eye, a shadow suddenly flung across the room and she whirled, almost crying out. It was at the window, and she glimpsed the dark branch of the tree as it moved in a sudden night breeze and she flew back across the room on tip-toes to halt at the window. The big oak tree rose up, its branches all but touching the window and Valery knew she had found her answer. That was Tansy's escape route. It was simple, so terribly simple. She'd just opened the window, reached across to the tree and climbed down.

Tansy had indeed been there at the glen, alone or not alone, but she'd been there. If she had an accomplice it would have been quite easy for her, Valery mused as she stood beside the window. Tansy could have held Fred Wheaten's attention while someone else crept up behind him to kill. But not Labat, and not anyone else here. Everyone had been somewhere doing something. Valery let a silent sigh of despondency rush from her. It was one more certainty that couldn't be proven. Tansy could have escaped from the room unseen, very certainly had done so, but she had no proof. The girl started to turn away from the window when Tansy sat up in bed suddenly. Valery dropped to her knees, making herself small in the dark square just below the window line. Tansy glanced around through eyes that were but half open, a figure more asleep than awake, and then fell back onto the bed, turning on her side at once. Valery held her cramped position, feeling her knees stiffening until she heard Tansy's breathing was deep and regular again. Finally she rose and crept to the door, slipping outside and letting her breath rush from her there.

She returned to her room with the one, the only absolute certainty clutched to her. Somehow, Tansy had to be stopped.

CHAPTER SIX

She woke early, her night spent on the edge of wakefulness, and saw the morning sky blue, felt the air already touched with the chill of fall. She put on slacks and a cardigan that was both light and warm. From the window she peered at the stables and waited. The wait was short as Labat appeared, turning the corner of the stable and heading for the house. She moved to the door and opened it, tiptoeing to the top of the stairs to listen. She heard him come inside and she waited, mentally following his soundless footsteps until she heard him in the kitchen, running water and taking down dishes. She crept down the stairs and edged herself behind the bottom of the stairway as the gaunt figure appeared with mop and pail. She watched him go into the east wing of the house with his cleaning equipment and she slipped out the door, closing it soundlessly behind her.

Running, she crossed the open space between the house and the stable, darting into the stable and past the wildeyed chestnut before he had a chance to start pounding his hooves. She saw the small wooden stairway at the rear that led up to the room above and she went up the steps two at a time. Below, she heard the big chestnut restlessly moving in his stall, aware of the stranger in the stables. The mare, *Mana,* and the other horse had begun to move, too. The door to the room upstairs was open and Valery entered without pausing, the inverted V of the ceiling giving the room more size than it really had. Work clothes lay scattered about, an unmade bed against one wall, a lamp, table and dresser against the other. A few magazines were strewn on the table and the floor. She swept the top of the dresser, paint-peeled and faded, with her eyes and then opened the top drawers. The first ones held a collection of string and old screws, tape, pliers, a hundred odds and ends and she rummaged through them carefully despite her haste. The earring would have stood out like a marigold in a swamp. She went through the other drawers, and then the pockets of the trousers on the bed. In a closet she found more clothes and shirts and went through those quickly.

A collection of cigar boxes held only loose change and fishing hooks. A cigarette box on the table held buttons. "Damn!" she hissed. "It's not here." She left the room quickly, going down the steep steps backwards. She didn't think he'd have carried it around with him till he could meet with Tansy but that's what he obviously had done. The horses were noisy, the chestnut starting the pattern of pounding his hoofs. It was still early and he would wake everyone, she knew. She flew past him and out into the morning air, edging around the far side of the stable, away from the windows of the house.

"It wasn't there," the voice said and she whirled to see Tansy standing beside the bushes just in from the far end of the stables. The child was dressed in a one-piece coverall, her blue eyes disdainful, amused.

"He woke you and gave it to you," Valery tossed out. Tansy's smile was enigmatic. It was enough of an answer for the girl.

"What do you want with the other earring?" Valery questioned, not bothering to keep the cold anger from her voice. Tansy shrugged. "You can't deny they ever existed now, or that they weren't yours."

"What do you want from me, Tansy?" Valery asked. "A promise to forget what you said to me down at the bogs?"

The enigmatic smile turned into a grimace of derision. "That doesn't bother me. No one will believe that, anymore than they'll believe you didn't kill him."

Valery held to her line of attack. "But they might. You can't risk that, Tansy."

"I can risk it. They won't believe an accused murderess."

"Then why don't you go to the police now?" Valery pressed, searching for a weakness, a soft spot in the child's icy composure. "What are you waiting for?"

"I can wait until they come around. It's more fun this way. When they come the best part will be over," Tansy said calmly. Her smile was ice-water, assured, cruel. The best part, Valery repeated silently. That was it, the cat-and-mouse, psychological torture, the child's own brand of sadism to cap off her counter-move. Valery felt the fury seething inside her. Tansy was a vessel of venom, utterly evil, and deserved to be destroyed as one would destroy a deadly germ. Only as the child walked off did Valery feel the pain in her hands and, looking down at them, she saw the deep marks where her nails had dug into her palms. She turned and walked away quickly, stunned by the depths of her own feelings, horrified by the hatred that spilled out of her. She walked blindly, trying not to think or feel. It didn't work, of course, as her mind raced in headlong flight. All her thoughts about Tansy turned to one place, every conclusion turned out the same. The child was absolute evil. She had to be reached; she had to be stopped before she did any more harm and Valery alone—if anyone—could stop her.

She halted suddenly, spotting the roofline of the abandoned old mill, and the round form of the huge waterwheel. How appropriate, she reflected grimly as she strolled toward it, the big waterwheel coming fully into view. A place for death and a favorite spot for Tansy. They went together and she could understand now why the child had been so icily composed and unaffected that afternoon. Valery halted in front of the hanging door to the abandoned mill, standing in the shadow of the waterwheel and then, drawn by an unexplainable force, she went inside. Some of the Van Dyne affinity for death rubbing off on her? she wondered idly. Inside the dank, musty mill the waterwheel at the one end stood silent, the horsefly still encrusted on the one paddle. The walkway alongside the wheel where she had fallen stretched invitingly to the narrow stairway, which was hardly more than a ladder, at the far end. She stepped on it and moved along the boards, stepping carefully, testing each step this time. The boards where she'd fallen were still hanging, leaving a gap for her to step across. Finally she reached the narrow spiral of wood steps.

She started up them, holding onto the thin rail, which trembled under her touch. She followed the spiral of the steps until she emerged at the top into what was a small loft, probably once used to store excess sacks of grain. It smelled of closed, unused spaces and small lines of dust ran along the edges of the floor. A narrow, horizontal window stood at the far end of the small loft and she walked toward it. As she did so she saw the small heap of papers in the corner nearest the window. A blanket, neatly folded, also filled the corner and frowning, she saw the field glasses on top of the blanket. Valery's frown deepened and with the toe of her shoe she poked into the heap of boxes and papers. Her frown deepened as she found the remains of cracker boxes, the foil from cheese wrapping, the end of a roll of salami. A handful of paper cups rolled from the collection of waste. Someone had been living up here. Her hands trembling, Valery picked up the field glasses and went to the window. Putting them to her eyes she scanned the landscape from the window. She was high enough to see over the rise and fall of most of the land and in the distance, through the trees, she could see the squatting shape of *Verdelet*. Moving the glasses to the left she could see the road from the house, dipping out of sight for a while and then coming into view again on the rise that marked the end of the hollow. She let the fieldglasses sweep on along the road and suddenly she halted, her lips opening in a soundless gasp. There, before her eyes, were the silver birches alongside the road, brought clearly visible by the field glasses.

Valery turned from the window, lowering the glasses as she did. This was how Tansy had known of her meetings with Fred Wheaten. Someone had lived up here, watching her every movement. But who? Certainly not Labat. He had been at the house, living in his room over the stables. Tansy? Had she been up here, perhaps for weeks before appearing at the house, with Labat bringing her food? It was not improbable, but it was impossible to understand. It made no sense. It hadn't even the excuse of self-protection which accompanied Tansy's ruthless amorality. Valery put the field glasses back on top of the blanket and went down the steps as fast as she dared. After edging along the wooden walkway, she rushed outside into the cool wind. Suddenly she was frightened, more frightened than when her entrapment in murder had become clear to her. That, sick as it was, was the result of the depraved workings of a twisted mind. This child of absolute evil had her own rationale. But this fitted no pattern. Suddenly she knew she had to flee, get away from this place. But running would only lend final evidence to Tansy's story to the police, she knew. And once the story was told, the damage would be done, to herself and to those she loved. Yet fear could be a weapon as well as a burden, Valery mused grimly. As she hurried back to the house, her mind formed a loose plan of action. She needed more time, time to think of how to get to Tansy, time perhaps to go home and find other means of help. She would try to buy time. The child's icy assuredness had to be shaken first. She would flee, and leave the child a note, Valery decided, a short note, cryptic and veiled enough to make Tansy pause. If it worked, she would have time to plan what was best. If it didn't, nothing really would be lost. Tansy's trap was quite complete. But it was worth the try. The broad brushstrokes of desperation painted her mind. She had to flee. Her discovery at the abandoned mill was past trying to understand, and a new fear had come with it. Valery realized how much more crippling the fear of the unknown is than that of the known.

As she reached the house, she saw Tansy's golden head near the rhododendron bushes, and the anger that by now was a part of her flared up. She was glad because it helped steel her determination and reinforce her conclusions about the child. Tansy was beyond helping. She needed to be removed from society. Anything less would permit her to go on to more monstrous things. Whatever other strange forces stalked this hollow of land, Tansy was somehow the vortex of evil. The knowledge had sickened first but had turned into something else. Hatred, she had called it at first. Others would call it that too, perhaps—but it wasn't, Valery concluded. It was monumental indignation, a gargantuan moral wrath at what had been done and what was being done. It was ironic that Tansy should speak of how others deserved death when it was she who deserved to be destroyed. Valery found herself frowning at her thoughts, frightened by the coldness of them and she wiped them away quickly. It was this place, this whirlpool of excesses. It affected everything and everyone.

Glen appeared as she reached the door of the house, his hazel eyes serious, searching her face.

"Everything all right?" he asked and she nodded. "When I heard you'd gone walking alone I was worried about you," he said. "You've a way of stumbling into things, it seems, and there's a murderer loose someplace around here."

His eyes were gentle and she realized his concern was real. "Thank you, Glen," she said gratefully. "I'm fine."

"Good, but I don't think you ought to go walking around alone in lonely places," he said. "Not till this thing's cleared up."

"That won't be too long from now," the voice cut in and Valery turned to see Tansy standing there, an assured smile touching the perfectly formed lips.

"I don't know about that, Tansy," Glen said. "Sheriff Huxley called Bob this morning and told him it would be another two days at least before they came here for questioning. He called to warn us not to admit any strangers. It is somewhat isolated here."

"Two days," Tansy said, her voice sing-song. "Even three. They'll go fast." The cool blue eyes stared a moment at Valery, who made no attempt to hide the hate in her own. "It must be hard to be a murderer, knowing each day might be your last one of freedom, the day you're going to be discovered."

The soft, assured smile stayed on her lips as she walked away. Valery's eyes narrowed as she watched the child go and then she turned to Glen. "Thank you for worrying," she said. "It was nice of you, very nice."

She brushed past him and went upstairs, afraid of kindness, tenderness suddenly. It didn't fit here, not now, anyway. It would gnaw at what she felt inside herself, undermining the ruthlessness she had to bring to bear. In her room she completed her plans. She'd go through dinner, facing down Tansy boldly. Then later, when the others had gone to bed, she'd slip away and walk to town. She'd find some place to wait there till morning when she would get the first train anywhere. She'd take only her small bag. The rest of her things could be collected later. She might well be hearing from Sheriff Huxley anyway. She went to the window and looked out. Bob was exercising the wild chestnut and she felt a warm smile grow as she watched him. Poor Bob, he wouldn't understand her leaving in the night. Not till later. Then he would know. Then he'd understand a lot of things. She thought of his bitterness last night and the strangeness of his words. It would all fall into place when this living nightmare was over. And then, then his electric vibrancy could set her afire again, with nothing to come between them.

She went downstairs, a sudden boldness, an arrogance of anger taking hold of her. She would spend the afternoon with Tansy, doing what she'd been hired to do. She enjoyed the wary look in Tansy's eyes, the sudden moment of uncertainty. "Yes, Tansy," she had said. "We'll do whatever you want to do." The child recovered quickly, the enigmatic smile taking over and they had played lawn tennis.

In the late afternoon Tansy went to her room and Valery fled to hers, drained and trembling in a rush of released nerves. She stayed there till dinner and finally went downstairs. Bob was polite, his face drawn, the bitterness still just beneath the surface. It was best this way for now, she concluded. Glen was his genial self and she wondered if geniality could be its own insularity, as much a mask as any other. It was an aberrant thought, she decided. Dinner was bearable mainly because she had made her decision, and was secretly secure in its strength. Tansy's smug, watchful amusement brought its own pressure but Valery let her eyes show only confidence. Dinner was nearly over when it happened, sudden as an exploding bomb. The shuttered windows flew open with a tremendous crash, a rush of air sending the drapes curling, almost blowing out the candles on the table. Valery heard her own scream of fright as the windows blew open and then, just as suddenly, the wind ceased but the room grew frigid. Shivering, Valery saw Bob and Brother Martin exchange glances. Tansy stared impassively at a flickering candle. The icy rush of air lasted only seconds and then, as suddenly as it had come, it was gone and the room was warm again. Labat noiselessly crossed to the windows and pushed them closed.

Brother Martin raised his wine glass and Valery saw Bob do the same. Tansy stood up as the two men rose, her luminous eyes staring straight ahead into space. "To Carlotta," Brother Martin said. The old clock in the corner of the room struck eight and Valery saw Glen's interested observance of the scene. Bob, taking his seat again, flashed a warm, enveloping smile at Valery, the first one he had given her not tinged with yesterday's bitterness.

"And to you, Valery," Bob said, raising his glass in a second toast. Brother Martin joined in and Valery didn't hide her frown. There was a strange cast to the toast, almost as when gladiators toast each other before combat. She pursed her lips at her own foolish thoughts. After Labat moved in to collect the dinner plates, Valery stood up.

"Time for bed, Tansy," she said firmly. "I think you've been up much too late these nights." She met the child's glance, staring her down. Tansy rose and said goodnight to the others and followed obediently from the room. It was working, Valery told herself. The child was unsure. She went up the stairs feeling Tansy's eyes on her. Opening the door to the room, she let Tansy enter first. Inside, Tansy turned, her round eyes narrowed.

"You're through, you know," Tansy said evenly. "You can't possibly win out."

Valery didn't reply. She turned down the black satin quilt and opened the window a few inches. "You're being a lot cooler than I'd expected," she heard Tansy say. "Of course, you're acting."

The child's cold disdain, so filled with assurance, bothered her, but Valery kept her composure. Maintaining her attitude was no trouble at all.

"Go to bed," she said, making herself sound unconcerned. Tansy's eyes stayed narrowed and Valery could almost see the twisted, calculating mind at work. She pulled the door closed after her and walked down the hall, putting down the rage that boiled inside her. Had she fooled Tansy at all, she wondered? Had she dented the child's contained assurance? Was the child also acting now? Fear added its voice to rage, an unholy harmony that frightened by its near-uncontrollableness. The child could bring out both at the mere sight of her now. As Valery went downstairs, Glen was waiting in the hallway, his soft eyes more searching then usual.

"What's bothering you, Valery?" he asked, the question both alarming and startling. Did it show that much, she asked herself instantly. If so, her bravado for Tansy had indeed been for nothing, a transparent charade the child had certainly pierced.

"What makes you think anything's bothering me, Glen?" Valery smiled. He half-shrugged.

"Little things, I guess," he said. "A look of trouble in your eyes, a kind of feeling I get."

"Don't let your imagination run off with you," she answered brightly. "It's really nothing in particular and everything in general."

"I know what you mean," Glen said. "It's this place, especially with what's been going on around here, murder and that sort of thing. This place gives me the creeps. It gets to you after a while."

"More than you know," Valery said, more grimly than she had intended. She saw the instant quzzicalness in his eyes. "I'm quite all right, really," she laughed. "Just a passing mood, that's all." His sympathy was inviting, an invitation she dared not accept.

"Well, be careful," Glen said and she glanced at him. There was a note of strength, almost command in his voice that surprised. But his face was open, characteristically bland. "Sometimes I think this place was well-named," he said, almost an afterthought.

"How do you mean?" Valery asked. "I thought it was some kind of old family name. I didn't know it meant anything."

Glen shrugged again. "It fascinated me when I first heard it," he said. "Bob, himself, said he had no idea what it meant. I got caught up with it, I guess, and kept looking into it. I found that *Verdelet* is the name for the evil spirit that acts as master of ceremonies at Satan's court. It also brings witches to the witches' sabbat, acting as a kind of devil's guide."

Valery's frown knitted her brow and she looked past Glen at the brooding excessiveness of the house, feeling the oppresiveness she had come to know so well. "What an odd name to give a place," she said softly. "But it does fit." In more ways than one, she added silently. It was a house to usher the tortured spirits on their way. Indeed, it had played its part in the consuming evil that was Tansy, she was sure. She glanced again at Glen. His quick, bland smile was typical. "I'll be fine," she said. "Good night, Glen." He nodded and she went past him and up the other stairs. Bob was in the library, his voice drifting out from the open door and she was glad he didn't come out seeking her. In her room she latched the door and set her final plans. She took the large shoulder bag she'd brought, emptied it and lengthened the straps so she could carry it over her shoulders without holding onto it. Then, working quickly, she jammed in her wallet, keys, panties and bra and a dress. A pair of shoes filled it to the top and she pulled the drawstrings tight and set it on the chair. She turned the light off in her room and pulled a straight-backed chair over to the window. Sitting down on it she fastened her eyes outside. She saw Bob cross to the stables, stay a little while and then return to the house. The light in the room above the stables was on and she could see Labat's figure through the window moving about. The moon went behind clouds and stayed there and the night grew pitch black. She lay down on the bed and made herself stay there, even though sleep was impossible. It was past midnight when the light in the window above the stable went off.

Valery got to her feet and went to the window again. The night was a little less black, the moon behind a layer of gray sky that permitted a faint halo of light. She pulled the window drapes together and lighted the lamp as she took a sheet of notepaper from her drawer, putting an envelope next to it on the table. Her hand was steadier than she had hoped for as she began to write. The note had to be short, and cryptic enough to put fear into the child. Valery put her pen to the paper and began to write:

> When you read this I will be gone. I know more and have more proof than you realize. I will contact you in a few days. It will be best for you to say nothing till then. I can help you or hurt you.
>
> Valery

She sealed the envelope, wrote the child's name on the front of it and turned the lamp off. If it worked she would have the time she needed to find a way to reach the child, or those who should know about her, or both. Opening the door of her room, she listened and was surrounded by the sepulchral stillness of the house. It was a silence she had come to know well. Leaving the door ajar she slung the bag over her shoulder and crept from the room, the note held tightly in her hand. She went down the stairs against the rail, stepping where the old wood was firmest. In the hallway, dimly lit by the kerosene lamp at the far end, she put the envelope on the small semicircular table against the wall. It would be seen at once in the morning, she knew. At the front door she grasped the doorknob with both hands and turned slowly, carefully, until the latch sprang open with only a soft click. She slipped through the opening and gently closed the door, not daring to push it and risk the harsh sound.

She moved to circle behind the stables. Hurrying across the lawn, she heard the whinny of one of the horses, alerted by instinct. She paused, waited, and then went on. She would pick up the road by circling around, cutting into it where it rose to mark the end of the hollow. The huge bulk of the house loomed up behind her and she hurried on, anxious to be free of it. After that she would find some way to force Tansy to admit the truth. The coldness of the night wrapped itself around her and she groped her way along, moving to the left, toward the road. The lack of a moon was both a help and a hindrance. She brushed against a row of bushes, realized where she was and hurried on, moving up the slope toward the road. She was nearly at it when she paused for breath and looked back toward the house. Her quick turn caught the movement behind her and she felt her breath leave. She stood absolutely still, listening, and then the sound of leaves being pushed aside reached her. Someone was moving against the bushes, coming toward her.

Valery turned from the road and ran back through the bushes, unmindful of the sound she made, heading toward the darkness of a line of trees ahead. Stopping for a second, she listened and heard the sounds of someone behind her in pursuit.

She ran again, faster, into the wooded section and she halted to peer out at her pursuer. The diffused light that managed to seep through the clouds showed the figure only as a shape, half-crouched, moving toward her and she caught a glimpse of long, loose arms swinging as he ran. Labat! Only Labat had that loosearmed gait. Had Tansy suspected her moves and sent Labat to watch the house all night? There was no time for conjecturing now. Turning, she ran through the trees to emerge on the other side of the small patch of woodland. Before her the rise that led to the lake was a smooth carpet of blackness and she started for it when suddenly she shifted, changing direction, racing along the edge of the trees. The sound of her pursuer came to her from a line almost parallel to her. She changed direction again, leaving the edge of the trees and running across the open fields. She thought of heading for the lake and the tall reeds there but they would afford no hiding place. In the still of the night they would rustle with every movement, betraying her at once. The field sloped upwards and she glimpsed a line of yellow flowers, almost white in the darkness, and she realized she was nearing the bogs. Valery ran faster, and she glanced back to see the shape moving across the open field after her, hardly more than a shadow in the night. She paused for breath, watching to see if the figure was tracking her by only her sound, but she saw him come on without pausing. Her eyes widening, she caught the dull sheen of something in the man's hand, a moment's light on the knife. Turning, she ran headlong across the ridge and down the slope toward the bogs. Tansy's problems would be solved another way if Labat killed her, Valery realized in horror. Another murder victim of the unknown killer. Simple and effective. Valery ran, felt her footsteps on softer ground and the mist on her face. She was at the bogs and the mists reached out to her as she stepped on the marshy soil. Tansy had said there was a way through it, which meant there had to be solid ground. She wouldn't try to find the way through but only a place firm enough to shroud herself in the fog. She stepped further, testing with each step, hearing the sounds of footsteps coming behind her. She sucked up mud as she stepped down, pulled her foot loose and moved to the left. Again there was the sinking trap of marsh soil and she moved further to the left. This time her foot felt ground that held, giving only a little as she stepped down on it. She moved forward, venturing a few steps on, enveloped in the swirling fog. On ground still holding firm, she dropped to her knees. She wouldn't dare to go further. To try would be to die perhaps in just another way. Forcing her breath to expand slowly, taking in small gulps of the fog-bound air, she waited in stillness and heard the sounds of her pursuer as he moved with mud-sucking steps along the edge of the bogs. He didn't know the path through the bogs any more than she did, Valery was relieved to realize. The footsteps continued, moving back and forth, each one making a vacuumlike sucking sound in the marshy soil.

Valery waited in silence, wrapped in the mist, refusing to shiver. The footsteps finally ceased sucking up mud at the edge of the bogs and she heard them move off, the sound of them pressing down resisting grass as they went up the slope. But the girl didn't move yet, not even after the sound had gone away completely. He could be coming back silently for another look, she reasoned, and she allowed herself only to stand and stretch her legs. Time had passed quickly, she knew, and it was deep in the night. Finally she moved from her small island of fog-bound safety. Sliding each foot ahead of her, testing each step forward, she made her way back the way she had come, only a few yards to the end of the swamp. It felt as if it had been miles. She became aware of the mist growing lighter around her. With unexpected suddenness it left her and she was at the edge, feeling unprotected, vulnerable. Her eyes blinkingly pierced the dark at the bushes and trees that lay ahead, looking for some movement. There was none, so she started up the slope, crossing the ridge of land and heading for the road. It lay almost directly ahead of her, she was sure. The line of tall, waist-high grass brushed her. She went along it, then turned at a sharp angle and went on, crossing the land where it dipped and rose again. The road was just ahead now, she knew, and as she hurried up an incline the row of bushes to her right ended abruptly. Their dark shapes were replaced by a lone, tall figure standing astride the road, waiting for the chance to strike.

Valery shrank back, behind the line of the bushes. The road curved away at this point, and the only way she could reach it was to move into the open. He would spot her then, of course. He had picked his spot perfectly, guessing that she must sooner or later go for the road. Undoubtedly there was another way to town but she didn't know it and to try and find it would be to give the shadowy figure another chance at her, one he probably wouldn't miss. He would have that soon anyway, her watch told her. There was hardly an hour left till dawn. Valery backed down the small incline, staying in the shadows of the trees and bushes. Far enough down she turned and ran back toward the house, staying in trees and shrubs wherever possible, running back to the relative safety of *Verdelet.* Finally the black outline of it rose up before her and she ran, this time crossing in front of the stables, to the front door still leaning unlatched. It swung open to her push as she rushed in. Snatching the note from the hall table she raced up the stairs to her room, locking the door behind her and falling on the bed, shaking in a rush of released tension. She had failed. The child had outguessed her, had been ready for the unexpected. She had won again, for this night, Valery admitted grimly. But only for tonight. There'd be no giving up, Valery told herself angrily. Tansy couldn't be allowed to go on. Too much was at stake, for herself, for everyone, those close to her and those not yet touched by the evil of the child.

She hadn't wanted to go to Bob but she would in the morning, she decided. She'd have him take her into town on some pretext or another. Once there, she would tell him what she was doing, leaving. She'd claim illness, nerves, anything. She would promise him whatever she needed to promise him. The time for conscience had passed. Only survival mattered. It would be but one more thing he wouldn't understand till later. She forced herself to lie quietly, not to think any further. The first hesitant light of the new day had already touched the sky when sleep overtook the girl and she lay, face down, her jet hair a dark halo around her head, as the night slipped away.

She tossed restlessly, staying asleep only because exhaustion held her in its grip. When she woke, the morning had reached its midpoint and she sat up with a fright, the pursuit of the night still with her. She pressed her hands into her face, wiping away the night, trying to plan her next move. Undressing quickly, she bathed and put on a heavy skirt and a sweater, hurrying downstairs to see Tansy outside through the hallway windows. The child was weeding the line of rhododendron bushes, pulling up the unwanted weeds and putting them in a small pail she held in one hand. As Valery passed the hall table she saw the cable lying open atop it and she halted to read it, a frown instantly furrowing the smoothness of her brow.

Regret to advise you of the death of Carlotta Van Dyne last night at Wilson Hospital. Time of death: Eight P.M.
Dr. M. Sheed

Eight o'clock! The words leaped from the cable and she felt the shiver run through her, almost as cold as the frigid blast that had seized the dining room. She wondered what strange forces touched this house. What unknown powers swept this place? Was Tansy a product of something more than Brother Martin's wild theories and some genetic aberration? It was ridiculous, she told herself. Once again the spirit of this place was seeping into her imagination, turning it into hidden corners of the mind. Tansy's twisted, warped viciousness, her evil in disguise, was terrible enough. It needed no strange, unexplainable obbligato of unnerving events. Turning from the cable she saw Brother Martin coming down the stairs, the long gray robes giving him the appearance of walking on air. He would look absolutely pious, she thought, were it not for those constantly restless eyes.

"Good morning, my dear," he intoned.

"I saw the wire," Valery said at once. "I'm very sorry."

The small smile was filled with just the right note of quiet acceptance, and he nodded gravely.

"Have you seen Bob?" Valery asked as he came down to her. "I want to tell him how sorry I am, too."

"He left early this morning," Brother Martin said and Valery felt her heart shrivel. "Things needed immediate tending to, I'm afraid."

"He left?" she echoed, dullness in her voice, numbing dullness. "When will he be back?"

"I don't know," Brother Martin answered. "He could be away for some days. Or he might possibly be back tonight. There's no way of knowing."

With another nod he walked past her down the hall to the library and she felt suddenly stripped of hope. Labat entered, leaving the front door open, passing her with his head down, going up the stairway. Valery went to the door and walked outside, unmindful of the sharp wind that stabbed at her. The grayness of the sky was no more bleak than her spirits. Tansy straightened up, halting her weeding to fix Valery with an expressionless stare. Valery's fingers tightened in fury as she met the child's eyes. Tansy's eyes turned sly, taunting.

"Did you oversleep?" she asked sweetly. Valery said nothing. "Have you thought about confessing?" Tansy asked. "I've heard they take confession into consideration."

Valery's mind raced, her icy hatred giving her new strength, like a battery suddenly charged. She had never realized that hate could be such an ally. Her eyes held Tansy's as she refused to let her despair become apparent to the child.

"How are you going to explain waiting all this while to tell them what you know?" Valery countered. "They'll ask why you didn't rush to them with my other earring right away."

Tansy's smile broadened, her composure unruffled. "I was afraid. You were watching me every moment," she replied. "I thought it best to wait till they got here and could protect all of us from you."

"You're sick, Tansy," Valery breathed through tightened lips. "You're sick, do you know that? You won't get away with this."

"Won't I?" Tansy smiled. "It's perfect. You know it is."

"I'll make them believe me," Valery said. "I'll find a way. You can't do things like this and get away with it. It won't work."

Tansy's laugh was almost too soft to catch, but Valery heard the derision in it. In despair she knew the reality of the situation. Tansy could get away with it. She had gotten away with murder already, cold, vicious murder, and Valery's weapons were meaningless. As she turned from the child's taunting stare Valery wondered if, indeed, she ever had weapons at all. Only if she could somehow get Tansy to admit the truth, was there a chance. If, somehow, she could make Tansy realize how sick she was—if she could only touch an inner spark of conscience, of normalcy. She looked back at the child and saw Tansy had returned to her weeding. It was an empty hope, wishful thinking, she realized. Tansy was sick beyond self-realization, with the terrifying shrewdness of the insane.

Labat came from the house carrying a suitcase and she saw Glen inside the hallway putting another bag on the floor. She went inside at once. "What are you doing?" she asked. "Why the bags?"

"I'm leaving," he said. She heard Glen's words first with astonishment, then as a clean wind blowing away her despair. "Oh, God, am I glad to hear that," Valery gasped. "I'm going with you."

Glen's eyes turning on her darkened and she saw his brow crease. "Going with me? Oh, I...I couldn't do that, Valery," he muttered.

"I'm all packed—all that I need for now, that is," Valery said. "How are you going?"

"Labat's driving me to town," he said. Valery's lips pursed for a moment. It wouldn't matter. The cadaverous accomplice couldn't risk anything with Glen there as a witness. "I'll get my things," Valery said.

"No," Glen said, his voice sharp and she halted in her move to turn from him. "I can't take you," he said.

"It's very important to me, Glen," Valery said. His soft eyes were looking uncomfortable.

"No, I can't," he said again, half-squirming.

"For God's sake why not?" she flared. "I can't stay here now."

"No, I can't. Bob's annoyed enough at me as it is," Glen said. "He woke me when he left and told me he was going away. I asked him if he'd mind if I left today and he said it was a good idea. I could see he was annoyed at me. He'd really be furious if I let you come with me."

His eyes flicked over hers and away at once, afraid to reveal the weakness behind them. "Please, Glen," she tried again. "I tried to get away from here last night by myself. I turned back, though."

"You what?"

She saw the astonishment on his face as he looked directly at her. "Yes, late in the night," she said. "I tried leaving but I didn't. I'm not going into why now. Just believe me."

His face was tight for a moment, even strong, as he was lost in his own thoughts. Then she saw the weakness come into it as his eyes flicked at her quickly, apologetically. "I believe you, it's just that I can't do anything about it," he said. "You and Bob have probably had some kind of falling out, over who knows what, and you want to get away from here. But I've got to work with Bob. I can't involve myself in it."

"No, you couldn't do that, could you?" she snapped coldly. His eyes mirrored a moment of pain and she didn't care. Tears of despair welled up in her eyes, mingling with those of fury, and she turned and ran up the stairs. At the top, she looked back and saw him walking out with his bag, Labat following silently. She had asked the impossible, she knew. We can't be anything but what we are. Glen was kind, attractive and weak. She went back down the stairs again, out to the doorway and stood there as he got into the old car with Labat. They drove off and she thought of how eerie it was to watch from the sidelines as your life, all your tomorrows, drives away from you. A terrible aloneness overwhelmed her. Turning away, she met Brother Martin coming from the library, absorbed in a book. For a fleeting moment she wondered what if she were to go to him and tell him everything she had learned about Tansy and everything else that had happened. She almost laughed aloud at the thought. Not only would he be the last person to believe her but his convoluted philosophies might make him enjoy the truth. Aimlessly, she wandered into the library, the sense of hopelessness beginning to assume a seemingly insurmountable size. She could try to run again tonight, she mused, but she knew better. Labat would certainly be on the watch again. This time she'd not get as far as the safety of the bogs. There was but one last hope and that was Bob's possible return. She understood now why people cling to forlorn hopes and clutch at straws. To hope is to live. They are inseparable; neither exists without the other, she told herself.

"Are we going to do whatever I want to do again today?"

Tansy's voice cracked the stillness and Valery spun around to face the pale-blue, coolly amused eyes. The child was standing in the doorway, mockery just behind the smile touching her face. Valery stared back at her. Perhaps there was no use pretending anymore but she had to go on. Pretense was no longer simply pretense—it was all she had left. It was pride, refusal, hate, hope, and in its own way, reality. Something beyond fear, more real than fear, ruled her actions with the child now. Certainly it was more than pretense to hate with a completeness that made one tremble.

"Yes, we'll do whatever you want to do," Valery said.

"I want to work in the garden till later," Tansy said. "After dinner, when it gets dark, I want to go down to the lake and hunt frogs by flashlight."

"Whatever you say," Valery answered.

Tansy's smile was pure malice. "Exactly," she said, turning abruptly and leaving. Valery watched her go to the small garden at the rear of the house, find a hoe and pail, and start digging. Tansy watched the girl with mocking disdain. Valery kept her face set, meeting Tansy's every glance with unruffled coldness. Inside, her stomach spun itself into a knot so tight she was almost sick. The game was too one-sided, she knew. She couldn't really match Tansy's composed assurance and she turned to face the sharp wind, the angry feel of it refreshing against her. It was driving low, gray clouds across the sky, whipping them on and its wildness caught at Valery, reaching into her to send a responding wildness inside her whirling about. She turned back and watched Tansy calmly digging in the garden, the picture of childish innocence.

The child needs to be exposed and destroyed, Valery heard her own voice silently commenting. Such utter deceit cannot be left to continue. Destroy her before she destroys you, Valery heard herself saying and she felt the muscles in her arms twitch and tighten. She stepped backwards, shrinking away from the horror of her own thoughts. What was happening to her, she gasped silently. To even entertain the thought was shattering and she had not only entertained it but had felt a righteousness to it. She caught the child watching her and a flood of fury wiped away the self-horror. Tansy was aware of the inner tortures she was going through, Valery realized. In her own way, Tansy knew and it was part of what she wanted. Sadism, torture, killing. Not just clinical terms used in textbooks any longer, but realities that had seized her in a grip from which there was no release, except one. The cold command floated through the girl's mind again and she struck it down again with a haste that was made more of terror than reason. She glanced around her helplessly. She stood alone, in the sharp wind, with nothing binding her and yet she was hopelessly trapped. She met Tansy's amused glance, unable to hide the desperation that had swept over her.

"What if I just walked out of here? What if I just walked into town and got the next train?" she flung at the child. "Labat isn't here to help you now. You couldn't stop me."

Tansy's smile was derisive, taunting. "I'd be on the phone before you reached the road," she said. "The police would be waiting for you when you reached town."

Valery turned away. Of course, she realized. It would be that simple. The question had been a wild thought, racing across her mind in desperation.

"Besides, you'd be a fool," Tansy said and Valery looked at the child with hatred. "You've nothing to lose by waiting. I might change my mind."

Valery kept silent but the child's words rang like a gong in her mind. Was this more of Tansy's sadistic psychological torture? Or was it a very real possibility? Hope, again, clutching at every shred of it. But it wasn't all that emotional. The child was sick, her mind twisted with its own icy self-torture. It had to be in conflict with itself. She could change her mind, perhaps try to strike the devil's bargain Valery first thought was her intention. Tansy's words were true enough. There was nothing to lose by waiting. Bob might yet return tonight. There was even that wild chance that she might still reach the child.

"I'm tired of this," Tansy said abruptly. "I'm going to my room. I won't be down till dinner."

Petulance, crossness, a sudden change of mood, Valery noted. The child's icy composure showed strain. Or was it only the momentary revelation of her disturbed psyche. Children were always subject to sudden changes of mood and whim. It was a part of their immaturity. But Tansy wasn't really a child. She was a living masquerade, death cloaked in beauty, consummate evil wrapped in the gauze of innocence. Valery followed the child inside and waited by the stairs till she heard the door to the room closed firmly. Then she went to her own room, restless, her nerves struggling to free themselves of their disciplined shackles. She stood at the window and let her eyes sweep the land, the clouds racing by, the grayness over everything. She gazed over the distant trees as the land rose and dipped and she imagined she could see the top of the abandoned old mill, the narrow window on the second-floor storeroom. It still didn't fit anywhere—not the spying on her nor the reasons for it. It still made no sense whatever. It had all the ingredients of plotting, of deliberation. But why, she asked herself. Tansy's ruthlessness had followed her admissions at the bog, the amoral insane reactions of the mad. Where was the connection between that and the field glasses in the old mill, with someone living there, spying on her? Yet there was a connection, of that she was certain. There were always connections. Our lives were made up of them, connections we neither saw nor understood. Yet they were there, sometimes revealed when we least expected them to be. Would these ever be, she wondered. She saw windows flying open and a dining room instantly turned frigid at the same moment an old woman died. What did it all mean? Coincidence? Was that the only meaning? Her coming here in the first place had its own meaning. She knew that now. Coming had been another opportunity to hurt, and she'd learned the terrible power of rejection. Brother Martin, for all his morbid philosophizing, was right about that. Those who rejected did kill, perhaps in small doses, a little at a time, but they killed. Of course, Tansy's sick mind had run away with the core of the truth in that and others had paid the ultimate price for it. What price would she pay for what she had learned, Valery asked herself. She stretched out on the bed and half-dozed in brief spurts as the day slipped into dusk, finally getting up as the darkness settled over the land. Glancing out the window she saw Labat crossing the lawn. She hadn't heard the old car return, she frowned. She must have been dozing when it had. Pulling the sweater off, she started to change before dinner, deciding on the slack outfit should Tansy still insist on hunting frogs by flashlight.

CHAPTER SEVEN

"It seems we are the only survivors of our little group, at least for tonight," Brother Martin said as dinner began, looking at Valery and Tansy. Valery threw a sharp glance at the cherub-cheeked face but it was benign, gracious.

"Survivors?" she echoed. "Isn't that an odd choice of words?"

Brother Martin expanded his smile. "Perhaps," he said. "I only meant that the others have, for one reason or another, fled our company and so we are the survivors. You know, my dear, there are many ways in which we survive. Sometimes we do so because we fight our way to survival. Other times we are merely left to survive. It can be both positive and negative."

"But terribly important, isn't it?" Valery said grimly. "To some people, at least."

"To all of us," Brother Martin said almost gently.

"Not as all important to everyone," she answered. "Honor, right, justice, those things are more important to some of us."

"Rubbish," he said. "Survival is man's most basic instinct, the time when he must put the end before all else." His eyes twinkled as they moved restlessly across Valery's face. "An eschatological concern, again, I'm afraid, a finality that outweighs everything else."

Valery lapsed into silence but for the second time in one day she found herself agreeing with the ex-friar's thoughts, a phenomenon she would have thought quite impossible. Her eyes swept Labat as the man's gaunt figure passed the table silently but his eyes stayed averted. Tansy's luminous orbs were not reluctant to meet hers and there was infuriating self-assurance in them. Brother Martin carried on with his philosophical musings and she was glad for the blandness of his thoughts this night, which were quite easy to tune out. Finally dinner ended.

"I'll get the flashlights," Tansy said, rising at once.

"You still want to go frog-hunting by flashlight?" Valery asked. Tansy nodded, turning to hurry from the room.

"I used to love to hunt them by night when I was a boy," Brother Martin said. "They freeze when the light strikes them. They're easiest to catch then. But of course, one mustn't be too slow or they recover and leap away, a human parallel."

"How do you mean?" Valery questioned.

"We all freeze when we're struck by the totally unexpected," Brother Martin said. "Whether we recover in time to act governs whether we survive or not."

Tansy appeared with two flashlights and a net, changed into slacks and a short jacket. Valery picked up the sweater she'd brought down with her, slipped it on and followed the child into the darkness. The night air was cold, the moon fitful, darting out from behind the low clouds still wind-driven in quick flashes of white light. The child walked on ahead, not using the flashlights, the spun-gold hair a faint beacon in the dark. They crossed the ridge and went down the slope toward the lake. The wind blew and Valery shivered, feeling small and alone. Ahead of her Tansy paused, waiting for her to catch up. As she did, she saw the amusement in the child's eyes—a cruel, sadistic light—and Valery felt her hate for this little package of towering evil. As Tansy went on, Valery mused darkly. What if there were another accident, just one more tragedy in the long line of similar tragedies that had beset the Van Dynes? What if Tansy were to drown in the lake, an accident in the dark, a deep hole just offshore, a stumble in the night? There would be no one to know, anymore than there was with the little girl from town that afternoon. This lake of death would welcome another. Its unmoving stillness was understandable now. It was a place of mourning, silent and motionless.

The water of the lake came into view, dark on dark, the cold wind leaving it unrippled, blowing over it without seeming to touch the surface. Tansy was kneeling at the edge of the water. It would be so easy, Valery thought again and she shrank back into herself, horrified by her thoughts. She should never have agreed to come down here with the child. This place harbored death. Tansy's back was to her, the net in one hand, the flashlight in the other. Valery felt her arms twitch and she stepped backwards, suddenly afraid of things she could neither see nor hear. Tansy had switched on the flashlight and she was bending forward at the edge of the water, her feet partially covered by the water.

It would take so little. A sudden shove, taking the child by surprise. Valery felt her hands suddenly wet with perspiration. It would put an end to everything that faced her, to Tansy's diabolic entrapment, and to Tansy. She would be free and the child would no longer be a menace to society. Valery wrenched her gaze from the child's back, sick at her own thoughts, wanting to still the persistent threnody of death that filled her mind. She stared into the dark, watching the brief glances the moon threw down at them in between clouds, lighting the waving reeds and the trees surrounding the lake. Survival. The word leaped in her mind. Man's most basic instinct, Brother Martin had said, the finality that outweighs all else. She shot a glance at Tansy, at the slowly moving flashlight as it threw its pencil beam along the shore. That the child deserved to be destroyed was no longer even questionable, Valery told herself. It must be done, in one way or another she had already told herself and now she said it again. It would happen sometime, of course, but the mind shrank from thinking of what horrors the child might do till then. No, now was the time, before she did any more harm. Valery pressed her eyes closed and held her hands to her face, swaying, feeling nauseated. Tansy's voice cut through the night, startling.

"I'm not waiting any longer," Tansy said and Valery opened her eyes to look at the child. Tansy stood with the flashlight laid on the ground, its light diffusing upwards and outwards enough to touch the perfect symmetry of her face. "I just thought I'd tell you," she added.

"You're not waiting any longer for what? I don't follow you," Valery said.

"For the police to come around," Tansy said matter-of-factly. "I'm calling them tomorrow."

Valery felt the cold bands tighten inside her.

"Why the sudden decision?" she asked quietly.

"I'm bored with you, with all of this," Tansy said coldly. "It's time to end it."

"Tansy, listen to me," Valery said. "You need help, Tansy. You're very sick. I can help you."

Tansy smiled. It was icy condescension and Valery felt her teeth rub against each other, her hands clasping and unclasping. She stepped toward the child. She had to try to reach Tansy. It was the most important thing of all now, the urgency of fear in it.

"Tansy, you told me how you felt about being rejected. The little friend of yours from town, you wanted to help her—remember, you wanted to do something nice for her but she rejected you. You wanted to be nice to the cat but she refused to let you. Remember how you felt?"

"I remember," Tansy said. The pale eyes narrowed but the tantalizing, infuriating smile stayed. The child was an inhuman little monster, a demon in disguise.

"Then don't reject me," Valery said. "Don't turn away. Let me help you. You need help, Tansy. Come with me and tell the others what you've done."

Tansy laughed, a peal of pure mockery, stopping as quickly as it had begun. "You're stupid," she said. "Weak and stupid and I'm tired of talking to you."

"Damn you!" Valery felt herself exploding, all she had held back tearing away inside herself. "Damn you. Why did you say you might change your mind?"

"I didn't mean it," Tansy said, the luminous eyes unearthly in the diffused light from the flashlight.

"Why did you say it then?"

Tansy laughed. "Just to see your face. Just to let you hope for a little while longer. It was fun and it worked. I knew it would."

Valery leaped forward, her fury coursing through her like electricity, her hands reached out, grabbing Tansy's arms, shaking the fragile-seeming, cold-steel form.

"What is it you want, damn you?" she screamed. "It's not because of what you told me at the bogs, you said. Then what is it, damn you?" She was shaking the child like a sack of grain and she made herself stop, her hands still digging into the child's arms. Tansy's eyes were pinpoints of ice again.

"I wanted to, that's all. I wanted to and I did."

The answer, senseless, was a slap of its own, all the utter insane sickness of the child coming to the fore, immovable, unreachable.

"You can't go on. I won't let you," Valery said. The child had to be destroyed. It was the only thing left now.

"You can't stop me and you know it," Tansy shot back. Valery felt herself shaking as though she were a leaf about to be torn away by a storm. "You can't do anything to me," Tansy said, her laugh echoing again in the night, defiant, infuriating. Valery felt her hand come up in a sidearmed blow that struck Tansy full in the face. The blond head flew backwards as she fell into the water. Valery went after her, seeing only one thing now, knowing only one thing. The child had to be destroyed. It would solve everything. One quick stroke would solve everything and the world would be better for it. It was justice and nothing more. Tansy was struggling from the water now, swinging back, and Valery caught the blow on her forearm. She saw Tansy's face laughing and screaming at her, all that was threatening and hateful in the world. Finalities, the last things, Valery heard the thought as it raced through her mind. The end governing the beginnings.

"Tomorrow I'll tell them," Tansy was laughing. "Tomorrow you'll be finished."

It had to be. There was no other way now. Valery swung again with all her might, the blow sending Tansy down again, into the knee high water. "Monster-bitch!" Valery screamed and seized the child by the throat. Tansy reared backwards and Valery went with her, holding her grip around the child's neck. She threw Tansy down into the water, shifting her hold to the child's shoulders, pressing her under the surface. The spun-gold hair floated outward, then Tansy shook herself free and came up. Valery reached for her again, her hands closing around the child's neck once more. She stared at Tansy's translucent pupils. They glowed, but not with fear, nor with hatred. They glowed with triumph. Valery felt her hands go limp and she stepped back from the child, looking down at her fingers, still stiffened in their grasp. She looked at the child's eyes again. Triumph. Victory, it was still there, and even as she peered into the luminous blue eyes she saw the triumph fade from them and the frown appear on Tansy's face. "You can't stop me," Tansy called to her. "You're weak. I win."

Valery backed away, trembling, overwhelmed by horror. Turning, she began to run, first sloshing, spraying steps out of the lake and then on the ground, half-stumbling headlong flight.

"I'll win, do you hear. I'll win." Tansy's voice called after her, but she didn't glance back. She ran and the moonlight opened a hole through the clouds for her to see the tall, gaunt figure off to the right, moving toward the lake. She raced on, not caring anymore, knowing only that she had to get away from this dark and death-filled place. She shook in the cold wind and knew it was neither the wind nor the cold. The house rose up before her and she fell against the front door, pushing it open with a sob, racing up the stairs to her room, latching the door behind her. Safety? She couldn't know anymore. Was there safety anywhere when one is not safe from oneself, she wondered, as she flung herself on the bed. Her hands clutched the sheets, pulling them into little knots. She had almost done it. She had almost killed. She had wanted to kill and she heard her own sob, anguished, torn from her. God, she had wanted to kill Tansy. Give us enough motive and all the dark shepherds will lead us. She heard Brother Martin's words like some echo from the grave. They have their stewardship of our souls. We have all let them file their claims. They need only to wait to collect.

No, she heard herself gasp aloud. No, no, no. But could she deny it any longer? Was she just making empty sounds so she could live with herself again? Was she no better than Tansy, both ruthless amoral monsters under the skin? It couldn't be, it couldn't have happened. But it did and the girl groaned aloud in a tortured sob. Triumph, victory, the same expression that had sprung into Tansy's eyes when she had first slapped her in her room the other night. Valery lay, face pressed into the sheets, until finally she stopped quivering and the shattering horror inside her turned into a dull, numbing anguish. She hardly cared what happened now to her. She knew only that she had to call home before anything else. It was she who needed help, now, while there was still a chance, before the dark shepherds called to her again. There was a phone in the small study on the first floor, the one beside the library. She would call and then wait. Hardly concerned with what others could do to her, nothing seemed to matter anymore. Perhaps it never does, she mused. It's only what we do to ourselves that matters. It's only to whom we give over our souls, little by little, until we no longer own them.

Valery rose, aware for the first moment since she'd fled to the room, that she was soaked, her skin cold and clammy from the wet clothes. She stripped quickly and put on a dress after drying herself. Was Tansy still outside with Labat? Or had they both returned to wait for the morning? Perhaps, after calling, she would try to sneak out again and reach town. Perhaps Bob might yet return. Impulsively she took another piece of her notepaper and wrote quickly.

Dear Bob ....

    I want to see you the minute you get back. If I'm not in my room it means I had to get out of here. Please come and try to find me. I'll explain when I see you.

Valery.

She folded the note into an envelope with Bob's name on the outside, sealed it and took it with her as she opened the door. She'd slip it under the door of his room. The hallway outside was dark and she crept down the stairs, listening every few steps. It was only when she reached the main floor that she heard the voices, coming from the library, and she saw the flickering light of candles from the partially open doorway. Edging her way toward it, she halted beside the hall table, wondering if she could pass the doorway to reach the study without being seen or heard. Brother Martin's voice drifted from the library, soft but unyielding.

"It failed," Valery heard him say. "It failed." She felt the frown cross her brow. What had failed, she questioned silently.

"It almost worked," she heard Tansy's voice say.

"Almost isn't enough," Brother Martin answered. "You live. You are here, alive, and so it failed."

Valery heard her gasp and she pressed her eye to the edge of the door. A lone candle burned on the library table and Labat, Tansy and Brother Martin stood around it. The child was alive and something had failed?

"It was perfect in every way," she heard Brother Martin intone. "It would have been a masterpiece, even to the ultimate sacrifice. But it failed. You live."

Valery felt herself sway. It was impossible, and yet there could be no other answer. They had wanted her to kill Tansy! It was beyond sense, beyond all reason. They were all monsters, far worse than Tansy. Brother Martin's voice floated out again and she peered through the crack as she listened.

"I wonder why it failed," he mused aloud. "Of course, it was a failure only in actuality. It was successful philosophically. She almost killed. And now we must find a quick way to arrange things to look right."

Valery turned away from the doorway. The impossible had been real. She had been supposed to kill Tansy. She leaned back against the wall, quivering, and her leg struck the table. It moved, only a fraction, but the scraping sound was explosively loud in the stillness of the hallway.

The sound of footsteps from the library was instantaneous. She darted for the front door. She had almost reached it when she felt Labat's hands on her, one long arm circling her neck, whirling her around and she cried out in pain. The gaunt figure flung her against the wall and she crashed with a numbing force. His hands were on her again, turning her wrist behind her back. "Bring her inside," she heard Brother Martin say and as her head cleared she saw that she was being pushed into the library. Labat flung her into a chair alongside the table and she looked up at the three figures before her.

"How much did you hear?" Brother Martin asked, his smile the same benign, lofty one she'd come to know.

"You wanted me to kill Tansy," Valery gasped out. "Why? Are you all mad?"

"I doubt that you'd understand, my dear," he said. "And you seemed so perfect for our purposes, too. It would have been really perfection in every way. Carlotta would have been proud."

"Carlotta?" Valery exclaimed. "She was part of this—this insanity—too?"

"She chose you for us, her last gift, you might say," Brother Martin smiled.

"I'm sorry it didn't work out right at the waterwheel," Tansy said petulantly. Valery's stare at the child was incredulous.

"You planned that on purpose?" she said. Tansy nodded offhandedly.

"Tansy's little attempt to do things her way," Brother Martin said. "Children are so direct. They abhor subtlety."

Valery's mind seemed to stagger. "First I'm a victim and then I'm made into a killer," she said.

Brother Martin smiled. "Correction. We didn't make you into a killer. You did that yourself, with a little interior help, guidance from all the dark shepherds that are yours and yours alone."

Valery stared at the man. He was mad, as mad as Tansy. They were all mad, all except Bob. Obviously they planned around him, seizing their opportunities when he wasn't near. "You must have death around you, is that it?" she asked. "Anyone's death, even one of your own."

"In a way," he said. "We were interested primarily in letting you *think* you'd killed Tansy. Labat was waiting nearby to bring her out after you'd left and apply artificial resuscitation." Valery's lips tightened. So that's why the man's gaunt form had been there in the shadowed brush. "Thinking you'd killed Tansy would have been enough to unhinge your mind," Brother Martin went on. "It would have been interesting to see what you'd have done then. Perhaps kill yourself? Or just become a shattered neurotic? Or you might have tried to claim uninvolvement. It would have been fascinating to watch you come apart then. You would have, of course. It would have merely been a matter of time."

"But what if I had killed her in the lake?" Valery asked. "Beyond any hope of reviving her. Surely you must have thought of that possibility."

"We did."

"And you were prepared to risk that? Tansy was actually willing to offer her life if it had to be just to destroy me? You're all absolutely insane."

"Insane? Oh, no, my dear. We are no more insane than anyone with a sense of utter dedication to his purpose in life. And so far as Tansy giving her life, you show an appalling lack of understanding of the beauty of sacrifice. It is the supreme gift to sacrifice oneself to one's purpose. And, of course, this would have been both perfect and supreme. But unfortunately, it has failed in its ultimate beauty and now you must be disposed of rather quickly."

"Another tragic accident?" Valery threw out. "Were all the others the same?"

"All the others went more or less according to our plans," Brother Martin said. "Except for an occasional mishap and even then, the finality was complete and rewarding. But now, with you, we must improvise."

He smiled, a tolerant, patient smile she had come to know too well and he turned to Labat. "What do you think, cousin?" he said. "Not another accident at the lake. Something different enough to allay any questions."

"The car?" Labat said. Brother Martin frowned.

"It would be hard to set up. We haven't any sharp turns or high cliff roads here. Besides, where would she have been driving at this hour of the night and why?"

Valery glanced at Tansy. The child was listening intently, obediently. Labat was frowning in thought again. They were discussing how to kill her as nonchalantly as though they were talking about the color of new drapes. The unexplained senselessness of all that had happened made her anger rise in a silent wave. She could not sit by while they did it. She would not let them have it their way. She'd not be another carefully arranged tragic accident for them. If she had to die, she would make them pay for it. With her anger exploding she swept her arm out, seized the candle and, leaping to her feet at the same time, thrust it into La-bat's face. She smelled the acrid odor of fire meeting flesh, and heard the man's guttural scream. Then the candle went out. The room plunged into darkness and she ducked under the loose-robed arms of Brother Martin as he reached for her and then she was running out the door and into the hallway.

"There she goes!" Valery heard Tansy cry, as she flung open the door and raced into the night. Crossing the lawn, heading for the line of trees, she glanced back to see first Brother Martin, Labat and then Tansy's golden head as they emerged from the house.

"Fan out," she heard Brother Martin yell. "Keep her between us. And just seize her. Don't play into her hands. We want this done our way."

Valery saw Labat go toward the right, Brother Martin to the left and Tansy plunge straight ahead. The girl reached the trees and cut to the right. Labat would be closest and she could see his gaunt form in the moonlight, moving in and out of the bushes. She saw him pause every few moments to brush the back of his hand to his face. The others were there, too, and she could hear them on both sides of her. She sank into a cluster of bushes and waited. Tansy's slender form came into view and suddenly a beam of light split the darkness. The child had a flashlight with her and the light made a sweeping arc, coming closer. Valery stayed in the bushes, tensing herself as Tansy moved closer, swinging the light in a semi-circle. In moments it would fall onto the bushes where she hid, Valery saw and she rose on her toes, waiting an instant more, and leaped just as Tansy swung the light toward her.

"Over here!" Tansy screamed just as Valery struck out, knock-ing the child's arm down. She grabbed the flashlight, twisted and pulled and it came out of Tansy's hand. Brother Martin was first at the scene, crashing through the bushes with his robes catching on the branches. Valery hurled the flashlight and heard it shatter against his head. The light went out and he roared a scream of pain. Labat was coming up from the other side as she raced away.

"After her, dammit," Brother Martin screamed. "I'm all right."

The road was ahead, Valery knew, and she set a turning course for it, suddenly coming upon a dense cluster of brush. She dived into it and crouched there, listening to the sounds of her pursuers crossing paths. They would soon realize she wasn't running, she knew, and double back for a more careful search. But she'd be gone by then, darting off in another direction. She glimpsed Brother Martin's robes flying as the moon broke through for an instant. She could only keep up this deadly game for so long, she knew. The moon broke out again, lingering this time. She saw Tansy's golden head as the child turned and started back, first to realize they had gone too far. The moon stayed out, filtered itself through a cloud and then was clear again.

Damn, Valery breathed. The moon would make her game end that much sooner. She saw shadowy shapes flitting through the trees, one to the left, the other the right. She'd lost Tansy for now. She frowned as she thought she saw another shape move, off to the left of the center and she peered at it but it was gone. The moonlight played tricks, casting deeper shadows. A shape disengaged itself from the trees, coming closer toward her, long-armed, crouching. That would be Labat. She rose and ran. He had circled around and no longer was between her and the road. She raced for the road and heard his shout to the others. She had been seen but she continued to run on a straight line. Another shadow moved to the left of Labat, the round figure of Brother Martin. There was movement to her right. That could be Tansy though she didn't glimpse the tell-tale gold hair. She ran, moving in the shortest path to the road. The shadow on the left took on shape and now there was no mistaking the cadaverous figure. He was still a distance behind and she saw she'd reach the road first. She'd head for town, slipping into the trees that lined both sides of the road. If she were lucky, someone might be traveling on the road. She was already at the place where it curved, one part leading into the hollow, the other part going past. The trees lining the nearest side rose up before her and she plunged into them, glancing back to see Labat coming nearer, then another figure of loose, flying robes crossing over to join him. She ran through the trees, parallel to the road, dodging tree trunks, then cutting sharply to emerge onto the road itself and race across it and into the trees on the other side. She halted, falling to one knee behind a thick oak tree trunk, her breath labored and harsh. Through the underbrush she could see down the road some ten yards and she saw Labat emerge from the other line of trees. The tall, loose-armed figure peered up the road, then down it, and Valery shuddered as she saw the raw flesh of his face, seared and red, making him look thoroughly like a creature from the pit of hell. Brother Martin came out of the trees to stand beside him and Valery saw him holding one hand to his side as he took deep breaths.

Labat pointed to the trees from which they'd just emerged, their voices muffled and Brother Martin nodded and plunged back into the opposite trees as she saw Labat turn and go into the trees on her side. Valery held her place for a moment longer and then, moving silently, dashed from behind the oak and out onto the road. There, without thick brush and tree trunks in her way, she raced down the road. She was nearly at the place where the silver birches stood and she glanced back. Labat and Brother Martin were still searching through the trees lining the road. If she reached the small curve just before the birches she might just round it without being seen. She glanced back. Her foot struck a dip in the road, and she stumbled forward, feeling herself go down, the loose stones and dirt sharp against her knee, the trickle of blood coming at once. Leaping up, she started forward again, taking another look behind her and this time she saw the small figure on the road, moonlight touching the gold hair, turning it into shimmering silver. She heard Tansy's scream and her lips tightened. Damn the child. She had seen her. Valery raced forward as the curve began just ahead of her. She could round it before Labat and Brother Martin caught up, she saw, and as she fled around it she plunged into the trees on the right side of the road. A small gully appeared and she crouched down in it behind a line of hobblebush vines, their thick, looping branches an ideal cover.

She heard the sounds of their footsteps as they neared and then she heard another sound—hoofbeats pounding on the road. The horseman was coming up at a fast gallop, the hoofbeats sounding like thunder in the night, a welcome, wonderful sound to the girl. She rose and ran into the very center of the road to flag down the night rider. As the horse rounded the curve she recognized the big wildeyed chestnut at once and the broad-shouldered figure in the saddle. Her heart soared and she felt her legs grow weak with sudden relief. She cried out, a half-sob, halflaugh of deliverance. He had found her note. She waved both arms at him as the horse galloped toward her. The others were nowhere to be seen, perhaps still on the other side of the curve, perhaps quick to take refuge in the trees when they saw Bob approaching. The big chestnut neared and she called out to Bob, the relief in her voice making it a tremulous, uncertain thing. Her lips were still parted when she saw him hit the horse with the reins and the big chestnut raced forward, atop her now at a full gallop. Her frown was not half-formed on her brow when she saw that the horse was not stopping, no reins pulling him in. In the last moment left to her she looked up at the rider and saw Bob's strong face tight, his lips pulled back in an angry grimace as he bent low in the saddle. She tried to leap aside but it was too late. The onrushing horse, aiming at her with careful deliberation, struck her as she dived and she felt the shattering pain of the blow as she was sent sprawling, hitting the road and rolling over twice. When she halted, her head dazed, clouded, she half-rose to one knee, her instinct for survival taking over. She shook her head and cleared it enough to see the horse turning, coming back at her. The horse loomed over her and she saw Bob flick the reins again and the chestnut reared up on its hind legs. She heard the scream of shock and betrayal that tore from her throat.

"Bob! Oh, my God!" Her cry rang out in the night, a last cry of defeat and monumental incomprehension. The horse's hooves came down, skull-smashing, body-crushing blows. Valery rolled, feeling the thud of the one hoof crash into the ground. The second one grazed her shoulder, sharp shafts of pain digging into her and she cried out. Rolling over, she saw the big chestnut rear up again and beyond the massive forechest, Bob's face looking down at her. How handsome he is, she thought incongruously as the horse poised to strike again. The sharp, cracking sound split the night in two, interrupting, demanding attention. Dimly, Valery realized it was a shot. She saw Bob's face twist open in pain and as he pulled back on the reins, the horse whirled, coming down a foot away from where she lay. A second shot followed and she saw Bob grab at his shoulder, then topple from the saddle in an unreal, slow-motion tableau. There was movement to her right and, sitting up, she saw Labat and Brother Martin rushing up, Tansy's spun-gold head behind them. Then from the trees directly opposite her the other figure ran and she caught the dull gleam of the gun in his hand. The figure raced to her and, looking up with eyes swimming, head swaying dizzily, she saw the quietly attractive face, the soft, hazel eyes. She was dreaming, she told herself, the whole thing a terrible dream but the hand on her shoulder, firmly tender, was real and she felt her lips soundlessly form the name Glen.

He nodded and whirled and past his crouched form she saw Labat racing toward them, a knife upraised in his hand. Glen's arm came up and she saw it move convulsively as he fired, one shot, then another. She saw Labat clutch at his right leg, fall, then come up again, the cadaverous face a mask of insane hatred. Glen fired again, his last two shots, again at the onrushing man's legs.

Labat collapsed once more and in horror, Valery saw him pull himself up and then Glen was on his feet, rushing from her. She saw him bring the gun butt down in a swinging blow as Labat threw himself forward with the upraised knife and then the gaunt form lay still on the ground, Glen standing over it. Valery looked past and saw nothing. Brother Martin and Tansy had vanished and as Glen came back to her, she nodded with her head to where they had stood.

"I know, they've run off," Glen said. Valery saw the big chestnut standing quietly beside Bob's figure.

"He'll live," Glen said grimly, following her glance. "So will Labat. I wanted them alive, able to talk."

Valery felt her strength draining from her. "I don't understand. I don't understand." Her eyes closed, the world turned into something swimming in blackness and she knew no more, only dimly aware for a last moment of Glen's arms around her.

CHAPTER EIGHT

Valery's eyelids moved slowly, as light and warmth made their way through her slowly waking consciousness. Her eyes opened and she saw the ceiling of the room, the books lining the walls and the ornately carved shelf endings. She was in the library, on the leather sofa. Starting to sit up, she felt hands gently push her back. She turned to focus with some effort at the figure sitting on the edge of the couch. The quietly attractive face swam into view and she fell back, her breath escaping in a long sigh. Beyond Glen's hand and shoulders she saw other men moving about, in and out of the room.

"It's all over now, Valery," Glen said. His soft eyes, still soft, had a new strength in them. All that had happened swam in front of her, all the terror, the shock, the incomprehensibility of it, and only one thing sprang into her mind with sickening, horrifying clarity.

"I tried to kill her, Glen," she heard herself saying in a whisper. "I wanted to kill her. I almost did it."

"I couldn't get there in time," Glen said. "When I reached the house you had already left with Tansy. Of course, I didn't know where you'd gone. I could only see that Brother Martin was alone in the house."

Valery pulled herself up one elbow, her violet eyes dark with puzzlement, "I don't understand any of it Glen, except for what I tried to do and I don't really understand that. Or maybe I don't want to," she said. "Why did you come back? And with a gun? Why did they want to kill me? It's all a nightmare."

"I'll give you the pieces and you'll understand quickly," Glen said. "You know already about Tansy. You found out things there on your own that I, or I should say we, only suspected. You see, I've been working with Bob in his office for a year, as I told you, but the job was taken purposely. I'm a psychiatrist specializing in forensic medicine. I've worked closely with police agencies for many years. The number of tragedies that touched people connected with the Van Dynes had been a subject for some discussion among the Canadian and American authorities. Of course, they seemed nothing but pure tragic incidents. Yet they bothered us because we received a letter from the sister of Kenneth Van Dyne's wife."

"Tansy's mother, the girl who murdered her husband and killed herself," Valery injected.

"Yes, Tansy's mother. Just before the tragedy she'd sent a letter to her sister which the sister finally turned over to us after she'd read about the stableman and the New Brunswick girl. I studied it so long and so hard that it's part of me. The poor girl had written that 'there is an evil here, a terrible monstrous evil that is beyond believing and I've been made a part of it. I have a responsibility in it now that is more than I can bear.' "

"Tansy," Valery said softly.

"Yes. The sister thought the letter showed her sister was having an emotional breakdown. When the tragedy happened she was certain that was all it meant but then later she turned the letter over to us. We began to see a strange pattern to these tragedies. We worked very carefully, knowing we were in an area of shadowy supposition. Yet as I got deeper into it, I was certain that something very strange, frighteningly horrible, was at work here."

Valery nodded. "Not just Tansy," she breathed.

"That's right, not just Tansy," Glen echoed. "I took the job in Bob's office and played a role, a submissive, totally pliable personality, the kind that could be manipulated. It worked.

I saw Bob Van Dyne taking more and more interest in me and when he invited me to spend the time here at *Verdelet* I knew I was onto something. Of course, Carlotta Van Dyne had chosen you without his knowing that. It was indeed her last gesture, giving the others a particularly lovely victim for their own."

"That's why he said you were no longer necessary," Valery interrupted, her mind flashing back. She saw Glen's frown. "That night you interrupted us outside," she explained. "He was furious and wanted to send you packing."

Glen's slow smile was wonderful to see. "Yes, I made it my business to be at the wrong place at the wrong time," he said. "It was the only weapon I could use at the time."

Valery found a smile of her own, something she had despaired of ever finding again. She grew serious at once again, thinking backward quickly, as Glen went on.

"Finding the meaning of the name *Verdelet* was one of the things that started my psychological probe into the Van Dynes and the tragedies that surrounded them. Bob knew what it meant, of course, as he knew the meaning of the names of the horses, *Vodun* and *Mana*. *Vodun* is an occult religion practiced in the West Indies. One of its beliefs is that sickness is caused by the soul being possessed by an evil spirit. *Mana* is an occult term for a supernatural power that possesses things and people in varying degrees. I was certain we were onto something and I decided to make myself their next likely subject. Then, when I arrived, there you were on the scene. I had to play out my role to the end. I had to keep on, juggling more than I'd bargained for now. I had to keep on in case Bob did decide to use me, and to try and keep you from harm, too."

"I guess I really got in your way," Valery commented. "Then all the other tragedies were brought on by the Van Dynes."

"All of them, in one way or another. They used people as pawns in a devil's game of chess."

"But that time at the old mill, Tansy had planned to kill me outright," Valery said. Glen's lips tightened. "A bit of personal departure from the usual method that, thank God, didn't work. So the tragedy with the child from town, was apparently another instance of Tansy's wilfullness."

Valery recalled Bob's chastising the child after the incident at the old mill. The pieces were all fitting now, or most of them, anyway. The affinity for death, the excesses of the emotional and physical, the philosophy of the last things, all part of one pattern.

"And Tansy's mother," she said to Glen. "Something made the poor girl recognize the Van Dynes for what they were."

Glen nodded gravely. "Her letter told us that only we couldn't understand it fully," he said. "We'll never know exactly what it was that did it, what made her one day realize the truth. Maybe it was something Kenneth Van Dyne did, perhaps something done by one of the others."

"No, not really. That no doubt had its effect but it had to have been Tansy," Valery said, knowing in the way only a woman can know such things. "Suddenly the poor girl realized she had given birth to a monster, a child that carried in her an evil beyond help, beyond our understanding."

"Perhaps she realized she had only been used as a living incubator, a device to carry on the evil that was part of the Van Dynes' mission," Glen said. Valery's eyes looked at him, questioning his use of the word.

"Yes, mission," he said. "It was more than Brother Martin's philosophizing. It was born into them, their reason for existence."

"They're a totally insane family," Valery said. "Insane or something close to it. I keep seeing those windows fly open and feel that room grow cold when Carlotta Van Dyne died. Explain that to me, Glen."

"I can't," he said. Insane or *something close to it,* you said. Maybe it's that *something close* that we call insanity today. We're clinical today. We have to give things names which let them fit our modern concepts, whether they really do or not. At other times it would have been called other things, sorcery, witchcraft, the power to possess souls, to make others do their worst, supernatural powers. Maybe we should still call these things by them. The Van Dynes used every psychological device and every bit of modern knowledge of how our emotions work. But so did the ancient sorcerers, those accused of witchcraft, of having power over the minds and bodies of others. They merely used what worked then as the Van Dynes used what worked today. That's why the name *Verdelet* holds the key to their beliefs and their actions."

"The evil spirit that ushers witches to the witches sabbat?"

"Yes, but not only witches. The *Verdelets* ushered all those considered to have the powers of witchcraft though still undeveloped. Anyone who actually possessed extrasensory powers, or those who by luck were considered supernaturally possessed, was considered a servant of Satan. All such people were part of the fraternity of the dammed with the ancient *Verdelets* their ushers and messengers."

"And the Van Dynes were Verdelets in today's terms."

"Yes, ushering not witches to the witches' sabbat but ushering all that is base in man to the fore. Very carefully, very cleverly, they ushered people to their own, individual place of hell and damnation. They brought their victims to the point of hatred, rage, and murder."

"Then they really spied on me during the month I was here alone," Valery said. "Someone had lived in the old mill and watched me through the field glasses I found there. Tansy?"

"Probably," Glen said.

"Maybe there was someone else we don't know about yet," Valery offered. "I still can't believe that Tansy had the height or the physical strength to knife Fred Wheaten."

"She didn't," Glen said. "She got his attention while Bob Van Dyne crept up and killed him."

"Bob!" Valery's eyes darkened. "Oh, no, Glen. He was in the stables at the time, grooming *Vodun.*"

"Was he?" Glen said grimly. "Did you actually see him there?"

Valery felt her brow furrow as she thought back. Brother Martin had been in the house, talking to her, and Labat was with Glen in town. Bob was supposedly at the stables and she'd never suspected anything different as she skirted them. But it was clear now. He hadn't been at the stables but with Tansy. Glen's words brought her thoughts back.

"Leaving you alone at the house for that first month was not only a way to watch you and pick up things that could be of help to them. It was a way to let you gather inner tension. Each of their victims, those they brought to the point of killing, received a different conditioning."

"All the dark shepherds," Valery said in a whisper.

"All the dark shepherds," Glen echoed.

"They exist, Glen, they exist," she said, suddenly afraid again. "I tried to kill Tansy. I understand the look of triumph that was in her eyes now. It was the victory she wanted. But I tried to kill her. I did."

"But you stopped," Glen said gently. "You stopped. All the dark shepherds didn't win. The other forces won, Valery, the forces for good, you called them. They exist too. You proved that. You stopped."

"It was too close, Glen," she trembled, "too close."

"That other part of us exists. It always will, and there always will be spirits—those dark shepherds—waiting to seize command. But they can be defeated. We can defeat them, each of us in our own ways."

She fell back and the sharp pain in her side made her gasp. "Nothing broken," Glen said. "Just badly bruised. I took a look before you came around." His smile was quick and faded at once.

"I made believe I was leaving so I could come back after dark and keep watch. I could tell things were reaching some point of crisis," he said. "I could see it mostly in your eyes. When I jumped from the train after it left town I found that Labat had left the car for Bob to use when he returned. Apparently he was to come back for their celebration of having brought another tragedy to a close. He came back on an early train and luckily I saw him before he saw me. When I got the chance to work my way back to the house I saw Brother Martin alone inside and I felt absolutely helpless. I'd no idea where you had gone. When I saw you come rushing back from the lake I stayed put and watched. Then I saw you run out and the others chase after you. I followed along then."

"Then I was right, I did see another shape in the dark."

Glen nodded. "I had to wait, to let them commit some act which I could nail them for. I'm sorry it ended up in such a close call," he said. "I didn't expect Bob on that wild-eyed chestnut either."

Glen's hand touched hers and she curled her fingers up inside his. "It's all over now, Valery," he said. "We have them on attempted murder. The rest we know and we don't have to try and prove it. Most of it would be dammed difficult to prove anyhow. But they're finished, all of them. Tansy will be committed, too, and maybe she can even be helped yet. I doubt it, though."

"I doubt it, too. She's possessed now by more than can ever be undone. Those dark shepherds have her for all time."

"I'll finish up here and take you home," Glen said. "I've a lot of time to make up myself."

"Where?" she asked.

"I don't know exactly where but I know with whom," he said. She saw the quietly attractive face bend down and his lips brushed hers lightly. There was no weakness now, only a quiet strength. She gazed up at him for a long moment.

"You're entirely too good an actor," she said and saw his puzzled frown. "But I'll risk that," she added, lifting her arms around his neck. It made her side hurt but she ignored it. Some things are worth hurting for, she told herself.

www.ingramcontent.com/pod-product-compliance
Lightning Source LLC
Chambersburg PA
CBHW021222260626
47172CB00002B/552